The Rabbi
&
Princess
Harmonica

OTHER NOVELS BY JOE COHEN

BILLBOARDS
(1985)

THE MYSTERY OF EVE
(1995)

OAKLAND GLIMMER &
TALES OF THE WANT ADS
(2000)

THE MINEFIELD
(2002)

WANDERING CAIN
(2007)

The Rabbi & Princess Harmonica

A TALE OF HUMAN TRAFFICKING

Joe Cohen

REGENT PRESS
Berkeley, California

Copyright © 2012 by Joe Cohen

ALL RIGHTS RESERVED

ISBN 13: 978-1-58790-227-7
ISBN 10: 1-587890-227-3

Library of Congress Control Number: 2012944957

e-book:
ISBN 13: 978-1-58790-228-4
ISBN 10: 1-58790-228-1

First Edition

Manufactured in the U.S.A.
REGENT PRESS
Berkeley, California
www.regentpress.net

Women shall be the object of special respect and shall be protected in particular against rape, forced prostitution, and any other form of indecent assault.

Children shall be the object of special respect and shall be protected against any form of indecent assault.

Geneva Conventions

1

I was dismissed from the synagogue the same day my wife left me. Both my wife and the synagogue had found a replacement for me, Rabbi Herman Bladowitz of the sonorous voice and good looks. I wasn't dejected by this but relieved, for I'd cherished neither the congregation or my wife in the way they deserved, and fate had interceded to put things right.

I'd dutifully followed my father's path into the rabbinate only to find it was a mistake. I lacked true zeal, though I went through the motions convincingly enough, with professional demeanor. People seemed to take it for granted I was the real deal. As for Judith, I'd married her because I'd gotten her pregnant and it seemed the honorable thing to do. The baby girl was born premature, lifeless, and the shadow of that hovered gloomily over our marriage. There were no other conceptions.

My release from Jewish leadership came a month after I explained to a teenage boy I was counseling that I didn't believe in the personal God of the Bible, but something more akin to the "force," as alluded to in the Star Wars films. He relayed this to his father, a board member who set in motion the mechanism for my ouster and the ascendancy of Herman Bladowitz.

Judith and Herman had met six months previously, when he came to Berkeley from his native London to lead a weekend symposium titled "Whither Judaism?".

She'd not shown much religious piety until she was smitten by Herman's movie star handsomeness and the mellow British baritone he spoke in. She became newly spiritual, almost saintly, to the point of abstaining from sex with me (though not with Herman, as it turned out), and began following a strict program of *Torah* study, ritualistic observance, and preparing only kosher foods. She also got involved with Jewish charitable causes, performing *mitzvas*, or good deeds. I was jealous of his influence at first but let it go when I allowed I was indulging male pride more than genuine love.

There were ample opportunities to carry on affairs with women of the temple to calm my aggrieved morale, but such a course seemed futile and depressing, the stuff of bad novels, and I stayed clear of it.

In Judith's womb a new life formed, spawned by Herman, that would erase the ache of barrenness she had endured during our marriage.

Her defection to Herman after I lost my position caused

some scandal among the congregants, but they were mostly Berkeley liberals in a Reform synagogue who took the broad view and tolerated the situation. A few women asserted she was a shameless whore, but their voices were dimmed in a bemused chorus of acceptance and enjoyment of novelty.

The divorce was quick and non-rancorous, allowing Judith and Herman ample time to tie the knot so that their offspring could enter the world more or less legitimately. She asked no alimony and the judge granted us a simple division of property which brought enough profit from the house that I could live at least ten years without having to work. I felt liberated for the first time in my life, able to remove my mask and do what I wanted, and what I wanted was to be a nobody, basking lizard-like on the rock of creation.

Lest that seem unduly selfish in this dire world, I did have a purpose that could be considered socially useful, if only marginally, painting abstractions on canvas. I can't explain that except to say it's always brought me a sort of balance to form scenarios of no discernible sense with dollops of paint. I'm a dolloper at bottom, not a rabbi.

"Jake! No hard feelings?"

That was Herman's phone query the day the board voted to replace me with him, the day my wife did the same.

"No, no hard feelings, Herman, it's all yours, the whole schmeer. I hope it works out."

Judith had finished packing a couple of suitcases upstairs in our bedroom when he called. Rather than make an inane gesture of courtliness, I let her carry them downstairs by herself.

"Guess who." I handed her the phone.

"Herman, I'll see you soon," she said. "I don't want to talk now."

She stopped at the front door.

"No parting hug, please Judith."

"There's nothing more to say, is there, Jake?

"No, nothing."

She picked up the bags and carried them down the stairs to her station wagon. Fluffo, the neighbor's cat, approached and rubbed against her leg. Judith burst into tears.

"Goodbye, Fluffo."

She put the bags into the rear of the car and drove off as Fluffo and I watched.

After the property settlement with its windfall, I went to Australia. My brother Matt had been a practicing psychiatrist there for years, specializing in the emotional problems of children and adolescents and had achieved some renown after publishing a book, *The Trouble with Youth.* He had been lured to Sydney while a fledgling doctor by a generous start-up program offered by the Australian government in its drive to bolster the country's store of professionals. Within a year of his immigration he had a posh office and a hefty roster of clients. Matt found that despite the Crocodile Dundee bravado image, Australians have the same propensity toward imbalance as the residents of any other modern country, though they're less reverential toward psychotherapy than Americans are,

After five years of listening to the woes of adults he grew

impatient and shifted his emphasis to the young, who he felt were more amenable to treatment, with time on their side, and the flexibility to change their "scripts" before they solidified.

He took on a partner, Patrick Kyle, also a transplant from the United States, to deal with the adults, some of whom were parents of the younger patients. When they compared notes, it was obvious the neuroses of the parents were visited on their offspring like a hex. Connecting the dots, it was no surprise to find most of the children's problems could be traced directly to the hangups of their parents. When the parents were brave enough to look at this, Matt and Patrick conducted joint sessions with entire families that were very effective. Unfortunately, less than half the "grown ups" were willing to cooperate in that way, and their offspring continued to flounder. Still, it happened that with Matt's skilled guidance a lot of youngsters gained strength, and relief from their problems.

In the waiting room wall of Matt and Patrick's offices hung a large plaque inscribed with Socrates' dictum, THE UNEXAMINED LIFE IS NOT WORTH LIVING. Each new patient who was literate was required to return with an essay on what that meant to them.

I was two years older than Matt and had been his protector up to his second year of high school, when he took up martial arts at a boys club sponsored by the police department. He excelled at it and no longer required the intervention of an older brother. Our father had mixed feelings about his son taking on such a roughneck goyish sport, but saw its salutary effect on Matt's confidence and gave it his blessing.

He attended Matt's matches to cheer him on, and even became a boxing fan, watching the Monday night bouts on TV.

The Brody (our family name) residence was a three-story stone house overlooking Sydney Harbor in the amiable district of Potts Point. I was greeted by Matt's wife Sarah and their twenty-year-old son Zeke. They were tall, attractive people, dark-haired, brown-eyed, dimple-chinned, with natural smile curves on their mouths, a characteristic that let people feel relaxed around them. I hadn't seen them for ten years, when the family had last visited Berkeley.

"Matt appointed us special envoys to meet you," Sarah said. "He's tied up with work until this evening. Come on in. You're probably jet lagged, tired and wanting a bath. We've got the in-law apartment ready for you."

"Thanks Sarah. It's so good to see you both. You know, I'll just be here a few days, until I find a place of my own."

"Pshaw, Jake. Don't worry about that. You can stay as long as you want. We're glad to have you."

It seemed odd to hear a Jewish woman speaking with an Australian accent but, then, I had the same illogical reaction to hearing Asians, Africans or Aboriginals talk that way. I fantasized they'd naturally assert some native guttural structure by speaking differently, even though they were born in Australia. For what it's worth, Matt once told me he thought his American accent had helped build up his business because it made him seem sort of exotic.

Sarah was right about the tired. My fourteen hour flight from San Francisco had been a sleepless interlude seated next to talkative, active boys four and five years old, with their argumentative parents and an oft-crying baby daughter seated in front of us. By the end of the flight I felt as though I had a swarm of bees in my head.

After a shower I contemplated the harbor view a few minutes, lay down, and didn't regain consciousness until hours later when I felt a cold, wet rag on my face. It was Matt, playing one of our juvenile tricks.

"Well what do you say, man without a country, a temple or a wife? What do you have to say for yourself?"

I flung the washrag back and got him square on the forehead. Laughing, he raised his hands in the surrender position.

"Hey Matt. Here's what I say, 'Fuck all that stuff. I'm through with all of it.'"

Matt found that hilarious. He broke into laughter again, infectiously, and I joined in his bellowing guffaws.

"Good attitude, Jake. Fuck it indeed. What's done is done."

"Amen."

"So what now?"

"Now? I'm aiming for point zero, Matt, just zero. Gonna find me a studio with white walls. Gonna paint."

"That's it?"

"Yeah, that's my plan."

"Okay Mr. Zero. Come on upstairs. Sarah's done the Sabbath thing, candles, prayers, kosher meal. She's become observant the last couple of years."

"Yeah? How do you feel about that?"

"It made me a little nervous at first. You know I'm not a

believer, but I came to like it. She radiates warmth with the ceremony. I guess it makes me and Zeke feel warm too."

"You lucked out with that woman."

"Don't think I don't know it."

We were joined by Sarah's sister June who suffered from a version of autism, which in her case meant difficulty concentrating on spoken language.

Her face resembled that of a Raggedy Ann doll, though not as exaggerated as the features that used to be called "mongoloid," a label that must have been very annoying to Mongolians. During the week June lived in a group home with similarly afflicted people on the outskirts of Sydney. She earned a small salary working with a gardening team, an occupation she enjoyed and did well at. Weekends, she stayed with the family in the attic room. As we conversed during the meal, she looked around dreamily, occasionally contributing a comment such as "yes," or "wow," but was mostly silent.

After dinner we watched a German video, *Wings of Desire*, about an angel who wanted to live in clock time as a person and learn what human experience was like. June, though confused by conversation, had no trouble reading, and followed the subtitles avidly. She seemed to find the film fascinating, perhaps picking up some significance that eluded the rest of us.

After *Wings of Desire* we disbanded for bedtime. I slept heavily that night, pressed upon by the unfamiliar humidity of Sydney's atmosphere. In a dream, I was attempting to lecture the worshipers at my ex-synagogue as they ran around helter-skelter, throwing bibles at the walls.

A symphony of bird calls awoke me at dawn. I thought at first I was hallucinating when I heard a tapping on the window, and saw a yellow-plumed cockatoo staring at me, but no, it was there. I supposed it wanted a snack. I was going to like this country.

3

I found a suitable place to live a few blocks away, in a garden cottage that had been built by a Yemeni immigrant for his aging father, who died in Yemen before he could emigrate and take up residence. It was circular with large windows arched in Arabic style. The exterior walls were made of multi-colored blocks of stone set in a symmetrical pattern and the interior walls were white. It was furnished elegantly with a leather sofa and chairs, a handcrafted oak dining set, Persian carpets on the tiled floors. A den with a sun roof had been intended as a prayer room for the father and it was there I would do my painting. Before we signed a rental agreement, I mentioned to Muhammad, the owner, that I was Jewish and asked if that would be a problem.

"Not at all. My father, bless his memory, was a just man

who believed the light of God was attainable for all. He would welcome you as I do. I sense you're a person of spiritual inclination, whatever your background happens to be."

"Thanks. I take that as a compliment."

"So, Mr. Brody, what sort of work do you do?"

"I'm a retired rabbi."

That brought an ironic smile to Muhammad's face.

"You seem young to be retired."

"The truth is I was fired, and that's how I came to be retired."

His smile widened.

"I see. Please sign on this, line, Mr. Brody, and we will have an agreement."

Zero was working out for me. I painted in the mornings when the light was good. The rest of the day I read, walked, explored various corners of Sydney. Friday evenings were Sarah's sabbath meal, a social island in the week that I looked forward to. Occasionally I had a twinge of conscience that I should be doing something more "meaningful," but it was only a twinge and it went away.

The King's Cross district was an easy walk from where I lived and I went there often, sipped beer at outdoor cafés and took in the lively mix of tourists, locals, prostitutes, pimps, transvestites, and hallway barkers touting exotic pleasures to be savored in venues a flight up or down from the street. Young backpackers from various countries ambled about, participating in the lively scene with the cheerfulness of youth. Shuffling by or lolling on sidewalks and benches were the inevitable homeless people, needy, scruffy, down and out. Contrasted to these were well-dressed middle class people scurrying in and out of the Kings Cross subway station on the way to or from work. There seemed to be a hierarchy among the pimps, sub-pimps, hustlers and various flunkies who earned a living off the sex workers of King's Cross. Those at higher levels were generally better dressed and coiffed than their underlings and exuded a certain air of authority. I would notice a boss speaking quietly and confidentially to a subordinate, who would then move off on some errand, such as keeping an eye on one of the prostitutes soliciting business on a side street. Those kinds of interactions came to seem ordinary as I got familiar with the ebb and flow of the neighborhood. Like the Tenderloin district in San Francisco, it was a magnet for ex-cons, junkies, mental defectives, runaways, the sort of people who faced life without much hope, surviving each day at the bottom of the social scale.

It was out of this imbroglio that Princess Harmonica came into my life one night, lying unconscious in front of my cottage door.

I recognized her as one of the young women from the street mix of King's Cross, memorable because she always wore a harmonica on a cord around her neck, like an amulet. She looked no more than eighteen or nineteen years old, was blonde, lean, Slavic looking.

I called Matt, he came over, checked her vital signs, noted a puncture mark on her arm, said she'd overdosed on heroin but would survive. We put her in his van, drove to his place and carried her into the in-law apartment. Matt injected her with a saline solution to neutralize the effects of the drug. In a while some color flowed into her cheeks, she moaned, uttered some words in a language we didn't know, tossed on the mattress.

"She'll be all right," Matt said.

A police sergeant and a patrolman showed up about ten minutes after Matt called for them, took some notes, asked if he wanted to let her sleep it off there. He said okay, and asked if they knew anything about her.

"She's been on the street for the last six months or so," said the sergeant. "We've never had to arrest her, so we don't even know her name. You know how laissez-faire this city is about the flesh trade. She always wears that harmonica around her neck. We've seen her hanging out with a pimpnik named Freddie. Locked him up on an assault charge last week and nobody bothered to post bail for him, which means he's in disfavor with his higher-ups. He'll probably have to do a year or two in jail. Made the stupid mistake of mugging a young law student, who's going to sink his teeth into a game of courtroom. If this girl has any papers, they're probably in the possession of whoever trafficked her from another country. We'll leave that in the hands of Immigration."

"Tell you what, I'm a licensed official of the court," said Matt. "I think I can take temporary custody of her and simplify all this."

"Right, I've seen you a few times, in the Juvenile section. If you want to interview her yourself and send in a report with a recommendation, that's fine, that'll work. Let me get the signatures of you two gentlemen, and we'll be on our way."

Late into the morning, Sarah brought breakfast to the girl and sat to talk with her. Matt had felt it would be more comforting to her to awaken to a gracious woman than a burly man with a beard.

"Who are you?" She asked.

"I'm Sarah. I live in the house upstairs with my family."

"Why am I here?"

"My brother-in-law found you outside his cottage last night. He called my husband, who's a doctor, and they brought you here."

"Am I still in Sydney?"

"Yes, this is a neighborhood in Sydney. I can't place your accent. What part of Europe are you from?"

"I come from Romania. Can I eat?"

"Yes, please do."

She wolfed the food down as though she hadn't eaten in days. The three cups of coffee she drank seemed to stimulate her communicative energy.

She spoke in a rush of words, watching Sarah as though afraid she might leave if she didn't hold her attention. In the course of it, Sarah learned the girl's name was Sorina, she'd lived in an orphanage in Bucharest from the time she was four years old, and had no memory of her parents. The supervisor of the orphanage told her she had been left there because her mother couldn't afford to care for her. Sorina's father had been trampled to death by a crazed horse the previous month. The mother had signed away all legal rights so that the orphanage could give her up for adoption without complications.

It wasn't until she was thirteen that anyone showed any interest in adopting her. A couple from Croatia inspected the scores of children in the orphanage and chose Sorina after being assured she was free of disease. She was characterized in the institution's report as a bright student who had learned French and English and was willing to work. It was also stated she was a gifted harmonica player. What was omitted was that she was often withdrawn, sometimes delusional, and maintained the fiction she was a displaced princess from a far-away country. Ms. Kabori, the supervisor, said she had never had to be disciplined for an infraction of the rules and had been very helpful in caring for the orphanage's tots.

The adoptive couple gave Ms. Kabori a substantial "donation" for the orphanage, and she saw to it that a well-connected acquaintance obtained the required government documents in just two days.

"I didn't like these people who adopted me," Sorina told Sarah. "I didn't like them at all, but there was nothing I could do."

It turned out the couple, Andrei and Bianca, weren't married but were flunkies for a syndicate that acquired children and sold them into slavery and prostitution.

As Sorina described it, her new "parents" took her to a rundown hotel on the outskirts of Bucharest. After a meal and some rest, Andrei told Sorina she was going to travel far away and have a career as a hostess. He said he was going to show her what would be expected of her. Bianca left the room.

Andrei told Sorina that being a hostess meant being nice to men and giving them physical pleasure.

"No! No!" she cried. "I don't want to!"

"Calm down and relax," he said, "and it will be much easier for you."

He pulled her down to the bed.

"No, no, please! I don't want to!"

"You're going to find out whether you want to, or not."

He raped her, muffling her screams with his hand.

She lay in a horrified stupor throughout the night, weeping.

The next morning he raped her again, and left the room. Bianca entered a while later, barely in time to prevent Sorina from leaping out of the window.

When they arrived in Zagreb that night Andrei's boss ordered a henchman to take him to the basement and strangle him. Andrei had been told to deliver a virgin, a special order from a wealthy Middle Eastern businessman.

5

Some 80 members of Temple Adam and their guests heard an Israeli author read from her novel based on the phenomenon of prostitution in the Holy Land and its connection to organized crime. A summary of the events of the evening was emailed to me by Bekka, an elderly congregant who remained loyal and thought I should be kept in the loop. I preferred that the loop remain in the past but didn't want to squelch her friendly gesture. Her email read:

During the question and answer session after the reading, the inevitable, arch, question, came up: "What can we as individuals do about it?"'

That was posed by Morgan Hoff. You know, wrote Bekka, *the one who wears a sweatshirt that says WE CARE.*

I did recall him, a well-meaning guy always in the thick

of it, volunteering for committees, serving refreshments, raising funds, passing around get well cards. He worked as a warehouseman, had no family, didn't have much luck with the women of the synagogue. He may have been hampered socially by his blue collar status in a milieu of well educated high achievers. Bekka's e-mail continued.

The author, Leah Mazell, told of an Israeli organization called Time Anew that works to rescue victims, mostly female, from the international sex trade. These are her remarks, Jake, as well as I recall them:

"We recognize there are women who are sex workers of their own free will, and we have no quarrel with that. It's their choice, though I admit I have a hard time believing that's what they wanted to do when they grew up. We work with the ones who have been trapped into it. So one thing you can do, you can work with Time Anew, or seek out some other organization you feel compatible with. Money and volunteers are always needed. Another question I'm often asked is 'what are the dangers?' And the answer is that the organizations that do the trafficking don't like any interference. I'm sure your imagination call fill in the rest. Of course there's a risk; this is not a pursuit for someone who wants only to be happy and comfortable."

She addressed Morgan:

"'Does that answer your question?'"

"Yes, thank you."

Another questioner:

"What happens to the young women you find?"

"They're given medical and psychological care and the

opportunity to return to their native country. Most prefer not to return to their poverty stricken birthplace and be subjected to the same danger we pulled them out of. The problem with them remaining in Israel is we don't have staff to guard them twenty four hours a day from the pimps that controlled them, and the organization that originally bought or kidnapped them. So, we work with other concerned groups to locate them elsewhere, if there's no hope of safely reconnecting them with their family. They're seen as property and the property owners have no compunction about treating them severely. It's a vicious circle. Even pimps are human, and some have been killed after feeling some compassion, or falling in love, and helping girls to escape. An Israeli film director I know is presently making a film about an actual case where a pimp fell in love with one of his charges, took her to Cyprus and married her. They were discovered, he was brutally murdered. The girl was brought to a house in Nicosia and beaten, to teach her a lesson. The upside of it was a couple of policeman heard her screams, barged into the room, and rescued her. The thugs ran out of the room in a panic and the policemen, after a warning (so they claimed) shot them dead. The downside was, as dead men, they couldn't reveal who they took orders from."

"What became of the girl?"

"She's been in a mental institution in Tel Aviv ever since."

A final question:

"Why are the top dogs so hard to catch?"

"They're blended in with the world's power structures, the politicians, the armies, the business magnates, the courts, so that they're virtually invisible. The profits from their enterprises are laundered into the supposedly clean businesses that make the world go 'round. The best way to stop human trafficking would be end the demand for it, and I don't think that will ever happen."

That's pretty much it, Jake. Thought you'd be interested. Best wishes...Bekka.

In a follow-up email a week later, she informed me the synagogue's Social Outreach Committee, with my ex-wife Judith at the helm, agreed to sponsor a rescued victim of the flesh trade and see to it she got a fresh start in life. It was decided to avoid tribal chauvinism, a no-no among that tribe of liberal Jews, and find someone outside of Israel to sponsor. Bekka reported that Morgan objected to this, on the grounds that it was inane. "What's wrong with being of service to Israel?" he asked. "The Cosmitarian Church down the street has already staked out universal good as their domain. It's covered."

The committee decided Morgan's sense was good but not good enough, so it stayed with helping a victim outside of Israel.

I answered Bekka that I had no ideas or advice on the matters she related, and said that just as the temple had purged itself of me and my vague sense of God, I had purged myself of the temple, and therefore had no more interest in the goings-on there, but thanks.

 was awakened by a pounding on the door a couple of days after we had settled Sorina into the house of Matt and Sarah.

The questioner was a wiry, shaven-headed guy about thirty years old. He had the look of a street tough—a wispy chin beard, a moustache, a tattoo on his neck depicting a large-fanged snake. My reaction was he should have kept the hair on top of his head and shaved the hair on his face. The tattoo didn't do much for him either, though it may have given him gravitas among his peers.

"Yes?"

"Have you seen a girl around here? Blonde, about five-six. Wears a harmonica around her neck."

"Who are you?"

"Don't you worry about who I am, mate, just you answer

my question."

He peered at the interior of my place, obviously scanning for the girl. I was annoyed by the bullying tone of this obnoxious punk.

"All right, here's your answer. I don't know where any girl is and I don't like your manner. If you don't leave this property I'm going to call the police. You're trespassing."

A flash of indecision showed in his eyes and his attitude softened.

"Okay, mate, I was just asking, you know what I mean? Trying to find a girl, that's all. Acquaintance of mine said he saw her headed in this direction last night. She could be in trouble."

"Well she's not here." I closed the door.

Through the front window, I saw him reconnoitering the nearby houses, peering along the sides of driveways, under bushes, down an alley.

Matt called later to tell me Sorina was okay. She didn't have the multiple needle marks on her body characteristic of addicts, and her general health was good, except for chlamydia, a minor venereal infection that would disappear after some antibiotics took effect. He said he and Sarah had decided to let her stay as long as she liked, give her a chance to reclaim her life and figure out what happens next.

I told him about the character who showed up looking for her.

"You handled it fine, Jake. That guy was probably a sub-level pimp sent by the boss man to retrieve his investment. For the time being, we'll keep her in the house, out of sight. She seems pretty content. She's helpful to Sarah, and she and Zeke like having her around. She's surprisingly pleasant, considering what her life must have been like up to this point, the sordid things she must have had to do. If you see that character from the hurly-burly district who visited you, stay aloof, don't get into any conversations. He'll have checked back and assured himself the girl isn't with you or anybody else in your neighborhood."

I did see him a couple of nights later, standing at the stairway of a girlie club, joshing with a buddy and a very tall transvestite dressed in a mini skirt and shiny knee-length boots. A man of about fifty, wearing a thick black toupee, was leaning on the wall behind them. Occasionally he'd make a remark and the guys nodded respectfully. I was directly across the street having a coffee at a sidewalk table. If my visitor—I'll call him Tuffy—recognized me, he wasn't letting on. He was sporting a black eye, which could have been punishment for not finding Sorina, or maybe just the result of a fist fight.

As happened often, one of the prostitutes approached with a romantic offer. There were a variety of pitches, according to the sensibility of the seller. Hers was, "Do you want a good time? I'll give you the best price in town." Her accent was American or Canadian, definitely not Australian.

I said I was okay, but assured her she'd certainly be the one if I wanted a good time.

She giggled and wandered off, a dark-eyed, chalk-skinned brunette about thirty-five years old. Her beauty had been marred by a deep scar between her cheekbone and ear, likely a blade slash from some creepy customer or a thuggish pimp.

Wounds and their scars were an oft-seen aspect of the warp and weave of King's Cross. Injuries of the heart weren't so clearly marked, though their effects wafted through the atmosphere like doleful rays.

The toupeed guy who had given instructions to Tuffy drifted in my direction, stopped at my table and regarded me with narrowed eyes.

"How you doin', mate?" He took a seat across from me.

"I'm doing all right, and how about you?" I wasn't about to call him "mate."

"Well, I can't complain, you know? I've seen you around here a few times, thought I'd say hello. I'm proprietor of the Fascination Club, over there."

"The Fascination Club, hey? How's business?"

"Not bad, not too bad, but had a little problem lately. Lost a valuable employee, one of my entertainers. Got in a funny mood one night and wandered off."

"Sorry to hear that."

"Well here's the deal. She's a pretty young thing about nineteen. Slavic, with an accent. Wears a harmonica on a silver chain, like a necklace. We have a reward out for her, two thousand dollars. If you should hear or see anything about her, we'd be very glad to know. Her name is Sorina."

"I'll keep that in mind. What did you say your name is?"

"Mack Ruggles. And you?"

"Jake Brody."

"All right, then, Jake." He rose without offering his hand

and walked off with a limp that favored his left leg. When he got back to the Fascination Club the tall transvestite hugged him affectionately. He looked pleased and patted his/her buttocks.

7

I avoided King's Cross for a while after that, venturing into districts less intense but no less interesting, and made friends with some artists in a bar named the Frontback, perched at the base of Sydney Bridge. I'd been drawn to the place because it had an adjoining hall that served as an art gallery, a popular showplace featuring a revolving slate of fresh, original talent. Tourists taking in the harbor side attractions such as the opera house, ferry tours, and didgeridoo players, wandered in and paid good prices for whatever was hanging on the wall. To his credit, Martin, the proprietor, didn't pander to the perpetual rage for aboriginal art, though he featured some if he thought it exceptional. I showed him a few samples of my work and he invited me to have an exhibition complete with publicity and an opening night party. This was a well-attended event he staged every six weeks. I was flattered by the prospect but nervous about it.

"You want me to have an exhibition here?"

"That's right, man, you."

"I was hoping you might want to hang a couple of pieces, you know? But an exhibition. That's a big deal. I don't know if I'm up to it."

"Take it or leave it."

"How much time have I got?"

"Ten seconds."

"I'll take it, then. Thanks. But don't expect me to make sense if anybody asks what my work is about."

"No problem, Jake. Do like other artists: Talk gobbledygook and they'll eat it up. They'll think it's deep."

I'd been working energetically during my time in Sydney, and had completed thirty canvases that I thought were as good as I was capable of. If I were an art reviewer flapping out the jargon, I might have expounded they had bold color contrasts, free line flow and a sense of action suggestive of supernova explosions. On the periphery of each picture was depicted a lizard looking on as primordial witness. I was interested to read what snarky things the critics would have to say about that, probably something like, "The reptiles should be showing expressions of dismay."

It took place on a Friday night. Sarah cancelled the Sabbath meal so that she, Matt, Zeke and June could attend, help swell the crowd, and provide moral support.

A party atmosphere formed as people drifted in and gravitated to a table laden with finger foods, soft drinks, and wine poured by Martin's sculptress girlfriend Gina, a transplant from Italy.

I was intrigued by June's response to the paintings. Holding Zeke's hand and moving from one to another, she studied each with the absorption of a child pondering illustrations in a story book. I recalled her rapt response to "Wings of Desire," and wondered what she was thinking, or experiencing.

An overweight, pony-tailed guy wearing thick glasses and garbed in a tweed sport coat, jeans and polo shirt, approached and gestured toward a painting, waving his soda glass and jiggling the ice cubes.

"How long you been doing this sort of thing?"

"Since I was a kid, in one way or another."

He introduced himself as a writer for the magazine *What's Up in Sydney* and reached out for a handshake.

"The name's Art Mallek. I'm the events editor of *What's Up*. It's essentially a slick advertising mag that goes to all the hotels. There'll be coverage of this in the next issue but not to worry. We never pan anything. Our point of view is that whatever happens in the cultural life of Sydney only adds to its everlasting glory."

"Well, that's a comfort. And you Art, how long you been doing this sort of thing?"

"Been a year now. Not my first choice of a trade. I was teaching Creative Writing at the University. Turned down for tenure. It's a long story having to do with a government official's niece and what had begun as a harmless flirtation."

"My wild guess is, she was a student."

"Bingo. And here I am."

Sarah came over, looking worried.

"Have you seen June? I don't know what happened to her."

"She walked by here about fifteen minutes ago with Zeke. Seemed to be having a good time."

"Well I don't know where she is. Zeke told her to stand by the refreshment table and wait for him while he went to the bathroom. He came out and couldn't find her. I'm scared, Jake."

"Did you look in the women's bathroom?"

"She's not there either."

"Was she a wearing a blue jump suit, sort of a retarded-looking woman?" asked Art.

"Yes, that would be her."

"I saw her with a couple of men a while ago. I noticed one was holding her tightly around the shoulders, and they went outside."

"Oh God! No!" Sarah exclaimed.

Immediately, we ran outside and scanned the street. Sarah called June's name as I looked into all the parked cars. Matt and Zeke had seen us rushing out and were behind us.

"What is it?" asked Matt. "June? Did something happen to her?"

"She was escorted out by two men."

"What! How do you know?"

"A guy, a magazine writer, just said so."

"Sarah, go inside and call the police," said Matt. "We're going to search every doorway and every block around here.

Zeke, go with your mom and stay close to her."

"I want to help you find her."

"Do what I said."

Two cops pulled up in a couple of minutes, took a description of June, got statements from Art and the rest of us and sent out a city-wide alert. Soon, four more patrol cars arrived and the sergeant-in-charge ordered them to fan out in all directions.

"I want you to reconnoiter, check out every nook and cranny from here to King's Cross," he said, "and along the way ask if anyone's seen a short, brown-haired mid-thirtiesh woman with flat facial features, dressed in a blue jump suit, and accompanied by two suspicious-looking men."

The sergeant addressed Matt, "You're Dr. Brody. I remember you from a few weeks ago. Took a report from you about a young hustler who'd overdosed. Do you still have her in your custody?"

Matt hesitated a moment, answered, "Yes."

The sergeant—his name tag said "Griffin"—addressed me. "And you, it was at your doorstep, where she was unconscious that night."

"That's right."

"We can make a logical assumption about what's going on," Griffin said,

"Her pimp knows she's with the doctor here, and will offer a trade."

Sarah began sobbing loudly at this point, and Matt put an arm around her. "Easy," he said.

"Look sergeant, I might be able to expedite this, " I said.

"Some young hood who came to my place looking for her works for the Fascination Club. His boss is a guy named Mack Ruggles. He started a conversation with me a while back. That may be who engineered this."

"I know Ruggles. All too well."

He picked up the speaker on his car radio. "This is Griffin. Need Legal to get me a search warrant for the Fascination Club as soon as possible. Suspicion of kidnapping. Thanks, sweetie."

He called one of the patrol cars.

"Get to the Fascination Club right away, park in front and keep an eye on what's going on."

"We should have the warrant in about an hour. For now, I'd advise you to go home. Is that girl alone there tonight?"

"I called Sorina on my cell phone a few minutes ago," said Zeke. "She said she was all right."

"You'll keep in touch, won't you sergeant?" asked Matt.

"Anything, anything at all, comes up, I'll let you know. The best thing you can do now is just go home."

Sorina picked up the tension when we walked in. She'd been sitting with Buster, the family cat on her lap, and playing her harmonica. Before we entered, I'd recognized the tune, *Clair de Lune*.

"What's wrong? Where's June?"

"We don't know," said Sarah. "We think two men took her."

Sorina jumped up, in fright.

"Why? Why did they take her?"

Sarah shook her head.

"It's about me, isn't it? Because they want me back."

"We don't know anything yet," said Matt. "All we know is she's missing. The police are searching everywhere for her."

Sorina went to the front door, flung it open and started toward the steps. Matt and I intercepted, restrained her, and brought her back.

"No! Let me go! It's about me, not her. I know them! I don't want them to hurt her!"

I was surprised by how strong she was, struggling with us.

A remnant of the rabbi in me, the flock's shepherd who had lectured on *Fascist Mentality and Modern Victimizers*, was roused to outrage. How could people treat others in this way? I'd never come to terms with the lower-brained aggression of humans (including my own, I admit) and the horror caused by it. I'd concluded prophetic religion was but wishful thinking, a temporary palliative until humans evolved over the eons into sentient, civilized people.

"No, you've got to stay, " I said. "The worst thing we can do is cooperate with their bullying."

She stopped resisting, slid into a chair and looked around as though in a daze.

"June would be safe now if it weren't for me."

"There's something I can do," I said, "if the police don't find her."

"What's that?" asked Matt.

"I came to Australia with a ridiculous amount of money. It's money that drives them. If she's not back by morning, I can negotiate, work out a deal with those bastards."

"You think that wouldn't be cooperating?" said Matt.

"Not the way Sorina proposed. I wouldn't be giving them myself, just some damn money."

Outside was the sound of a horn, tires squealing, and a car speeding off. Sarah opened the living room door, looked out, and her face brightened in recognition. "June!" she called.

She was standing in the middle of the street, looking confused.

Almost as a chorus, we muttered, "Thank God!"

"I'll get her," said Sarah, scurrying down the stairs. She embraced June tightly and asked, "Are you all right?"

June nodded, yes.

"Who brought you home?"

"Those men."

"Did they hurt you?"

She shook her head, no.

"What happened?"

She tried to phrase something but gave up in frustration, as Sarah must have expected.

"Let's go inside," she said, taking June's elbow and guiding her gently up the stairs.

Once inside, June collapsed onto the sofa, covered her face in her hands and wept.

In the excitement of getting her back, none of us had noticed until then that there was a note pinned on her blouse. Zeke removed it and gave it to Sarah. She read it aloud:

"You know what we want," was all it said.

"Maybe you'd better take her to her room, look her over, see if they did any harm," said Matt.

"Yes." Sarah helped June to her feet, put an arm around her, and they went to June's room in the attic.

Sergeant Griffin brought Ruggles in for questioning several times and hectored him as aggressively as he legally could until an urbane lawyer turned up with a formal complaint alleging harassment, and Griffin's captain told him to cool it until he had some direct evidence. Griffin had wanted to put some worry into Ruggles which he hoped would spiral to a higher level after the investigation had turned up this interesting bit of information: The building housing the Fascination Club was owned by the wealthy, socially prominent widow of Ivan Rinkov, who had died the previous year. He had been president of a prestigious land development company.

The worry did indeed wend its way to loftier regions. Ruggles was transferred to a similar operation in Melbourne and replaced by the Melbourne manager, which made any long-distance hounding of Ruggles impractical without some clear evidence for an arrest.

A coincidence of the sort that transmutes scenarios in melodramas rolled in like a benign ocean wave.

Florence Rinkov sent me a cologne-scented invitation to a reception at her mansion honoring Sydney's "prominent artists." I was included on the list of notables, along with some movie stars, a circus clown, a miscellany of painters, sculptors, musicians and writers.

At the bottom, in elegant cursive, was written—*There are a lot of people who'd like to meet the mysterious and talented Jake Brody, including me. Missed you at your showing. Loved your work. Flo R.*

The Rinkov mansion was just a mile from my place, and I walked it, enjoying the balmy night air and the glimmer of stars as twilight gave way to darkness.

I'd expected a butler, high society style, but no, the door was wide open and the hostess spotted me and greeted me herself. More than greeted. She embraced me warmly, as though I were an old acquaintance.

She was perhaps forty, hazel-eyed, slim, a brunette with the sort of Mediterranean beauty one might see in a depiction of Dante's Beatrice.

"I know you're Jake Brody. I knew it right away, don't ask me how. I'm so glad you came."

"Well I'm glad to be here. Should I call you Flo, like on the invitation?"

"Yes. All my friends call me that."

"A nice sound. Like go with the flow."

She laughed, took my arm and led me through the entryway to a moderately sized ballroom that had been fashioned in the style of Imperial Russia. It was populated with seventy or so guests. In a corner, a string quartet was playing a chamber piece by Borodin. The walls were lined with paintings, and I saw that one of my own was hanging over a potted plant.

"You bought one," I said. "I'm flattered."

"It was a bargain. I think you're too modest in your prices. I would have paid more."

"I leave the money part to Martin. It seems to be a matter of guesswork."

"But tell me something, Jake. What does the lizard in the corner signify?"

"I was afraid somebody would ask that eventually. A suave answer might be, 'whatever you want it to,' but truthfully, I don't know. I just wanted a lizard there."

The corners of her eyes crinkled when she laughed, a very appealing characteristic.

She introduced me to a couple of writers chatting nearby, and excused herself to "play the room."

After a period of the usual well-intentioned socializing, guests sipping cocktails, munching canapes, drifting from group to group hoping to somehow warrant attention, the lights dimmed, and Flo stood before the quartet and waved her arms like a conductor. The musicians played a fanfare and the room quieted.

"I invited you here tonight because I think you're all wonderful," Flo said, "and you honor our city with your amazing talents. I'm so thrilled you came. You've already had Andy Warhol's 'fifteen minutes of fame' and I'm going to add just a few more moments to it. So for our next act, to ensure everybody knows everybody, we're going to shine the spotlight on each celebrity and each of you can take a bow. If you're with a spouse or a significant other, or just somebody you dragged in from the street, say their name and they can take a bow too."

As her assistant moved the spotlight from one luminary to another, Flo managed to recall their names without floundering, and each, along with their companions, received an enthusiastic flurry of applause. At the end of it, one of the actors took over the spotlight and shined the beam on Flo, who also got heartfelt applause, along with whistles and cheers.

She said, "Play!" The musicians, launched into *Tales of the Vienna Woods* and couples began to waltz.

The woman knew how to throw a party.

At the appointed hour of midnight (as stipulated on the invitation) the reception broke up and people began to leave, after the appropriate hugs, handshakes, avowals of re-connection and exclamations of appreciation. I lingered behind.

"Jake. You're still here."

"I'd like to buy you a drink."

"What a good idea. But our little bar is right over there, and the drinks are free. Just a few minutes, until the musicians and the caterers are cleared out, and we'll have some privacy."

"Fine. I'll wait out by the pool."

It was more than a few minutes, but worth the wait. She came to the pool with a bottle of champagne and set it on a table, along with two glasses. She'd changed into a terry cloth robe which she removed, and under it she was wearing a bikini bathing suit. It adorned such a curvaceous body that I had to force myself not to stare.

"Are you up for a swim? There's a stack of clean trunks for male guests, all sizes, over there, in the cabana."

"I'll be right back, then," I said. "Don't go anywhere."

The musical laughter again.

We toasted our mutual health, swam a while, drank some more champagne, swam some more, finished off the bottle. I asked if it was okay to kiss her and she said, "Let's find out." It was definitely okay, as opulent as the delirium I'd felt at seventeen when I lost my virginity with a certain magical, hitherto unobtainable cheerleader. It occurred to me it could be dangerous to get involved with this woman, but the more exhilarating thought, "Who cares?" rushed in and swept away dull care.

"Did you put something in my champagne?" I asked.

"Like what?"

"Like whatever makes me feel this way."

"I feel it too."

"You know, I think we'd be more comfortable in your bed."

"YES!"

She got up and ran, exhorting, "YES! YES!" and I ran with her, through the hallway, up the staircase, and into the bedroom.

The Rabbi and Princess Harmonica

We peeled off our bathing suits and the rest is glorious history.

What to do with Sorina? That was the problem. She was virtually under house arrest until some matters were resolved, though she didn't seem to mind. It must have seemed a wondrous haven after the life she'd been forced to live.

Matt and Sarah decided to put June back in the group home during the week, when they saw she was miserable away from her gardening work and the sense of purpose it gave her. The state agency that funded the home agreed to post a security guard on the sites where June would be working for a period of six months, after which the situation would be reassessed.

The Sydney police cruised Matt and Sarah's house on a regular basis day and night as a message to whatever thugs might lurk, and kept up a more subtle surveillance on the various family members, as we came and went about our business. Matt had some influential friends in high places but then, so did the human traffickers, which brought to mind a graffito I'd seen on a downtown wall: PARANOIA IS THE ONLY VALID POINT OF VIEW.

Matt called one morning to inquire whether I'd do some counseling with Sorina. She'd asked him about it.

"She's gotten to be like family here, and she'd be more comfortable talking to you than me, about some things. I've become a kind of surrogate father. Sometimes it's easier to confide in a stranger than someone you're related to."

"I'm not really a stranger."

"No, but you're not around much, and she's fascinated you're a rabbi. I think she's looking for some sort of spiritual affirmation, something to balance out the misery she's been through."

"I may not be an ideal spiritual advisor, but I'll be glad to talk with her. How about we work out a set time, say a couple of hours a week, when she and I can talk in your garden?"

"Fine. For openers, how about an hour this afternoon, at two?"

"I'll be there."

"I don't want to impose anything on your conversations, but let me tell you she has a withdrawal pattern. It's a defense, an incipient version of catatonia. Sometimes she'll look away and be gone to some interior safe place. Just be patient. Saying her name can help to bring her back."

She was sitting on a bench under the gazebo playing a

melody on her harmonica when I arrived. It was an idyllic scene, the surrounding flowers, butterflies circling, the pretty young woman making music. She stopped playing and watched somewhat warily as I approached.

"Hello Sorina."

"Hello."

"What were you playing just now? I didn't recognize it."

"It's something I made up. Did you like it?"

"Yes. Could you play it again?"

She played a cadenza, stopped and smiled, the tension gone from her face.

"So how's everything going with you these days?" I asked.

"Well, I've been happy and sad too. Do you ever get sad, Mr. Brody?"

"You can call me Jake. Of course I do. Everybody does. There are times life doesn't seem to have much meaning."

She was quiet for a bit, but not withdrawn in the way that Matt had cautioned about.

"I don't really know what meaning is supposed to be," she said. "Is it a feeling?"

"Well, I'll put it this way. Whenever everything in your life is going well, and you feel good about yourself because you do things in the world that express you and help the world, then your life seems to have meaning."

"So it's a feeling."

"Some philosophers say it doesn't matter what you feel, it's how you're involved in the world, how you affect the world by your actions. Others say it's when you have the deepest awareness of existence."

"In the orphanage the village priest used to come and he told us the whole meaning of life was to love God and live by the teachings of Jesus. Do you think that's true?"

"I think it's true for a lot of people."

"Is it true for you?"

"No. In the Jewish religion I wasn't taught to worship Jesus, the way Christians do, but I understand how people would feel that way about him. He seems to have been a powerful, brilliant, caring person."

Sorina was quiet again. She tapped the harmonica gently with the tips of her fingers, as though it were a talisman.

"How long have you had that?" I asked.

She tapped it a few more times, and studied me, as though trying to gauge whether I could be trusted. I seemed to have passed muster.

"When I was nine, a rich woman from Bucharest came to the orphanage at Christmas time and gave every child a gift. This is what she gave me. I was so happy. It was the finest thing I ever had in my life. The other children got clothes or books or toys and they were all trading each other for things they liked better. Polo, a big red-headed boy who was a bully, gave me his kaleidoscope and took my harmonica but I didn't want his kaleidoscope, I only wanted my harmonica, and I screamed, 'Give it to me! Give it to me!' I never screamed like that before because I was a quiet person, and Mrs. Kabori came over and asked what was the matter with me, and I pointed at the harmonica in Polo's hand and I screamed, 'It's mine! It's mine!' She looked at me as if I'd gone crazy. She took the harmonica from Polo and put it in her pocket. Polo ran away before she could slap him, and Mrs. Kabori told me to go to bed without any supper, even though it was Christmas Eve. But I didn't. I waited outside her window, in the snow, until midnight, when she went to bed. I could see her crying when she was in bed. I tapped on the window, and she opened it and I crawled through it into the room. I asked her why she was crying, and she said it was because she was lonely. She smelled like wine. I asked her if I could have my harmonica, and she cried harder, and she said, 'Yes,' and she gave it to me. She hugged me and kissed me and gave me some candy and told me to go back to bed."

I thought any more conversation beyond that would be excessive. I told Sorina I liked talking to her very much and that I thought the best way to communicate now would be to just sit silently for a while.

She nodded, and we sat without words.

10

I let Flo know I didn't want to be her ongoing prince consort to all the events in Sydney's version of high society. This was after I'd accompanied her to an estate auction, a lawn party and a fashion show. I explained that while I had learned how to be sociable, I had never learned how to be keen about it. She was miffed, but possessed enough common sense and wit to see my point of view, and the grace to accept it. The lovemaking and the psychic connection between us was gratifying enough that my disinterest in being a social butterfly didn't presage a rift.

"But you will come to some things with me, won't you, Jake?"

"Some things, of course. Do you have a bowling shirt?"

Again, the musical laughter.

"It's okay, I wasn't looking for a house ape or a toady.

You know who you are, Jake, and that's fine."

That chat took place in my studio while she posed for a portrait wearing a caftan, with her hair unpinned and flowing around her shoulders. I was working on an abstraction of her that I hoped would convey a mystical sense of a biblical woman, a character like Sarah or Magdalene.

She had agreed to pose if I promised the portrait wouldn't have a lizard in the corner, peering at her.

"No problem. No lizard," I assured her.

Muhammad, my landlord, had stipulated in our rental agreement that I couldn't drink alcohol in my cottage or sleep with a woman there who I wasn't married to, and that I could not pose one in the nude. Those were acts that would have compromised his religious principles, and I signed on because the excellent abode was worth the sacrifice. The first time he saw Flo enter with me, as he was tending the garden, I assured him, "Agreement honorably in place." Judging from the appreciative way he looked at her, he may have pondered whether morality might not be too stringent a burden on reality.

During the posing sessions, the prohibitions only served to warm up our libidos, and at the end, we would drive hastily to her place for fervid or languid consummation, depending on our mood. There's nothing like prohibition, to make desire more desirable.

After one of those trysts we lay a-lollygagging, listening to the score of South Pacific on the stereo, watching the gauzy curtains move gently in the wind over open windows. I decided to broach a delicate topic.

"Flo, you know that property of yours, the Fascination Club?"

"Yes. It's one of several deeds Ivan acquired."

"And you know my brother Matt?"

"I do. I met him and his wife at a fund raiser for the homeless. Very nice people. I also met Matt at his clinic, where I underwent a period of psychoanalysis with his colleague Dr. Kyle, during a low period in my life."

"Well here's the thing, I want to ask you a favor about one of the young women connected with the club."

I felt her stiffen and her response was unexpectedly sharp.

"I don't have anything to do with them."

"I don't imagine that you do. But let me tell you a story."

I related how Sorina had showed up at my doorstep, the events following that, and her present seclusion. I told about the pseudo adoption, the initiation by rape, and her conscription into the sex trafficking trade.

Flo jumped off the bed, paced in agitation, walked to a window, parted the curtain and looked outside. She turned toward me, and her expression was angry.

"I know about human trafficking. Everybody does. Do you think I have anything to do with that? Do you think I'm some sort of flesh peddler?"

"No, I don't think that. I never thought that."

"Then why are you asking me about one of the whores?"

"Her name is Sorina. Please don't call her a whore."

"You've been playing me. Get out of here! Get out!"

"What the hell's the matter with you? Why are you

reacting like this?"
 "Just get out!"
 I got out.

11

On the far shores of America, in Berkeley, California, the Social Outreach Committee of Temple Adam heard a report on the increasing phenomenon of sex trafficking in Australia. It was delivered by my ex-wife Judith, the chairman of that committee. She read it aloud, verbatim, from a report on the Internet that had been garnered from one of Sydney's daily newspapers.

It had grabbed her attention when she recognized her ex-brother-in-law's name as one of the interviewed: "Dr. Matthew Brody, a well-known Sydney child psychiatrist and author, stated he had treated girls as young as twelve who had been forced into prostitution. He said they suffered deep psychological wounds along with the many venereal diseases they contracted, and that they bore scars and unknit broken bones from beatings inflicted by pimps and customers alike. He described the traffickers who enslave these youngsters as 'human garbage.' Asked if that was an unenlightened attitude to come from one who treats mental illness, he simply answered, 'No.' He said there are forms of evil that surpass the ability of even therapeutic professionals to feel compassion."

The newspaper interview was datelined two years before Sorina had turned up at my doorstep.

Bekka, the member of my ex-synagogue who I'd asked not to inform me any more about goings-on at the temple, broke her compliance to tell me about the above for an important reason. The committee had voted to send two members, Morgan Hoff and Judith, to Sydney to look into the matter of sponsoring some trafficked girl to a fresh start in the United States.

My reaction was intolerant, politically incorrect outrage. I didn't want my past to come stumbling goofily into my present in the form of self-satisfied middle class white liberal do-gooders, one of whom had betrayed me with a man more to her liking and one of whom was earnest and sincere to the point of being pitiable. I didn't want them, these doppelgangers of my former self. No. I went to the Frontback and got drunk. It took six tequila gimlets to get me properly soused and it was worth it, even though I got a black eye in a bar fight with the devil. At least I thought he was the devil, in the blurry haze through which I saw him. I had never been totally drunk before, and found it quite pleasant to have the world and myself devolve into incoherent fuzziness.

The Rabbi and Princess Harmonica

I woke up the next morning with a colossal headache, swinging slightly between two trees in a hammock in back of Martin's bar. He and Gina had somehow lifted me and covered me with a blanket, assuming I wouldn't roll off the hammock onto the ground. I was relieved to see I hadn't vomited on myself, as drunks will do.

The hangover convinced me I didn't have what it takes to become a bona fide full time alcoholic.

During the bus ride home a middle aged woman I was sitting next to rose abruptly, shot me an angry glance and moved to another seat. I supposed I was reeking of tequila, and my rumpled, unshaven appearance must have conveyed that I was a sodden, dissolute bum. Stepping out of the usual Jake role into this new but sweetly temporary self image was perversely satisfying, and I laughed, which earned me another angry glance.

I disembarked at the bus stop near my block and took a moment to tuck in my shirt and smooth back my hair in case Muhammad spotted me walking toward the cottage. Conveniently, his car was gone, and I wouldn't have to exchange pleasantries through a pounding headache.

The blinking light on my phone's answering device told me there were two messages. One was from Matt, who said he'd heard from my ex-wife Judith. She wanted information about sponsoring a trafficked young woman to the United States. "What the hell is going on?" his voice crackled on the machine. "Have you been in touch with her?" The other message was from Flo—"Let's talk."

I got Matt at his office after he'd finished a teenagers'

group therapy session, and explained the business about Judith, Temple Adam, the Social Outreach Committee, the lecturer from Israel, and how, according to Bekka, his name had popped up on the internet and become an inspiration.

"This is a very strange can of worms," he said. "Do you want her here?"

"Not at all. There's no way I want my past bleeding into the life I have now. Any ideas?"

"Well, one idea would be simply to tell her what you just told me. On the other hand, you wouldn't necessarily have to see her at all. Apparently it's me she wants to talk to."

"Yeah. You know, I wonder if this could be an opportunity to get Sorina out of her trap and into a new life."

"We're thinking the same thing, Jake."

"It's your choice, then," I said. "If you want to respond to her, go ahead."

"I know some people who could cut through a lot of red tape, deal with petty officials to get papers for her, re-establish her identity. It's something to think about."

I slept for an hour after talking to Matt, and returned Flo's call. She wasn't there, so I left a message proposing we talk the next day, explaining I was presently under the weather and needed repose.

12

Flo apologized for her abrupt behavior at our last meeting, and said she'd like to resume posing if I was willing to have her.

We resumed.

Our temporary rift had brought a change for the better in the way I depicted her on canvas. I'd been frustrated by a certain shallowness in the work, and resolved it now using shadows to convey a veiled, dark side of her character I'd glossed over before. The darkness evoked an interesting sense of beauty, dangerous beauty.

"So tell me about the girl, Jake. What's she like?"

"Like ethereal damaged goods, like an elegant mosaic that's been smudged."

"I know what you're saying. And what kind of help were you going to ask from me?"

I asked her to turn her face back toward the window, so I wouldn't lose an amiable play of light that was streaming through.

"I was going to ask if you had any influence with the club people who rent your property, to get them to leave the girl alone."

"Jake, you don't know who these people are, what they're really like."

"I have a good idea of who they are and what they're really like."

"Yes?"

"They're like every tyrannical bully since the beginning of time who's tromped on others to gain advantage."

She sighed and shook her head as though trying to shake off a persistent conundrum.

"Everything I tell you is strictly confidential. Okay?"

"Okay."

"My husband Ivan had a reputation as a social benefactor, a contributor to charities, a patron of the arts. He was all of those things, and the glory rubbed off on me, making me the social princess of Sydney. I confess I liked that, the life he provided for me. When I met him I was fresh out of college, engaged to a nice man who was a lawyer, and on track to lead a comfortable life in suburbia with children, a nice home, a country club. I went along one day with Emmett, my fiancee, to one of Ivan's building sites, where Emmett had to deliver a contract. When Emmett was distracted, Ivan slipped a piece of paper in my hand with a phone number on it. 'Call me,' was all it said. Ivan wasn't handsome in any ordinary way, but rugged-looking, charismatic. He conveyed a sense of power. I thought I'd throw the note away, but I held on to it, and the rest is history."

"Ivan did it for you and Emmett was out."

"That's how it went."

"You're leading up to something."

"He had a lot of connections with people in Eastern Europe. He was originally from Ukraine. When communism and the Soviet Union broke up, gangsterism moved in to exploit the control gaps. Ivan had been a mid-level bureaucrat in the export of Soviet goods, and his expertise in that made it easy for him to shift into the black market and make huge profits. After he became very rich he wanted to break away from the gangster elements, and he came to Australia."

Flo paused, turned to look at me, raised her eyebrows and shrugged, as to convey that what followed should be obvious.

"But the gangster elements didn't disappear," I suggested.

"No."

"And they wanted Ivan to help develop outlets for human trafficking, in the Australian Pacific region."

"I can't say things like that. I'm nervous to even be talking to you like this."

"How deep are you really into it, Flo? Excuse the probing, but are you seriously tied to it financially?"

"Ten months after our marriage, I gave birth to our son Jeremy. Two years ago, when he was nineteen, he got into a violent row with Ivan over his use of drugs. They were both hotheads when they were riled, and they were yelling accusations at each other. Jeremy called his father a glorified whoremaster and Ivan struck him and knocked him down. I'm certain Ivan's self-horror from that hastened his death; Jeremy hit his head against the corner of a doorway and suffered serious brain damage. He became virtually a vegetable, and no specialist, no treatment, including surgery, has been able to help him. We put him a luxurious sanatorium in Switzerland, where he might remain until his dying day. It costs a fortune. I go every two months to visit him. I think he recognizes me but I don't know. I read to him, hold his hand, give him what comfort I can, and he just stares into oblivion."

Flo began weeping. She propped her elbows on her knees and wept into the palms of her hands.

I didn't need to hear any more to comprehend that her lifestyle and her son's upkeep in that ritzy sanatorium depended on a steady and deep flow of income from shady sources. It was a bargain with the devil she hadn't made, but was keeping.

"What would happen if you cut yourself off from those goons who got Ivan into a stranglehold? The sale of your mansion would probably keep you going for two lifetimes."

That look of fear came into her eyes again.

"They have the mortgage on it. Ivan had used it to leverage money for a shopping mall he was building."

"So walk away from it."

"Jake, I don't know if you're terminally naïve, or just pretending to be. The point is this—they own me. Don't you understand that? I can't walk away. I can't do that."

"All right. Let's leave it for now."

"Thank you."

"You know what I'd like right now?"

"A kiss, Jake? Is that what you'd like?" I nodded avidly.

"Then come over here."

As our lips touched she jumped up in alarm, looking at the window.

"What's the matter?"

"It's Muhammed! He caught us!"

"What?" I glanced at the window. There was no Muhammed there.

Flo burst out laughing. "Got you."

"You got me."

We laughed uproariously. It felt good.

13

At first, Zeke and Sorina sat on the living room sofa and talked. As time went by, they held hands while they talked. Eventually, they fell in love. Sarah saw it developing and was disturbed by it, as was Matt. The pimp people hadn't made any moves since the night June had been abducted, and we feared what the next might be. Returning Sorina to the street was unthinkable, and also unthinkable was the idea of Zeke sticking his neck out and getting hurt. I was hoping Flo had enough persuasiveness with the whoremasters to get Sorina released, but that was iffy.

Zeke called and asked if he could join Sorina and me during our next conversation in the garden.

"Sure, if it's all right with her," I said. He put Sorina on the phone and she said that it was.

The Rabbi and Princess Harmonica

I told Matt about Zeke's request, and he surmised it was a good idea. "Zeke's twenty years old," he said. "He can think for himself. Sort of."

As I approached the garden next morning, there was the music of a guitar as well as Sorina's harmonica, Zeke accompanying her to the tune of *Mr. Sandman*.

He rose and embraced me as did Sorina, after a moment's hesitation.

"Thanks for coming, Uncle Jake," he said. "There are things we'd like to talk about."

"Yeah? So what's on your mind?"

"We want to get married."

"Really!"

They nodded in the affirmative.

"Have you told Matt and Sarah about this?"

They nodded "no."

"We wanted to try it out on you first," Zeke said.

"Well, I don't know what to tell you. You know, I probably have the same reactions your parents would have, such as, where will you go, how will you earn a living, and how do you know this isn't a temporary crush? Zeke, you're in the last year of university, and you want to do graduate work. What'll happen to your engineering career if you drop out to take some ordinary job?"

"It's not just Zeke's career," said Sorina. "I want to study, too, and become a teacher of French. We want to have valuable lives, not just play house."

She had a mature cast to her features I hadn't seen before, the visage of someone with purpose. I didn't doubt love could soothe a tortured soul, but could it truly heal it?

Zeke leaned forward earnestly. "If you're thinking about Sorina's past, the life she's had, I know everything about it. We're honest with each other. I know she's had mental problems, we've talked about that too. We can work through all the difficulties. I can transfer my scholarship to the university at Perth. It's far from here and it's safe. We can work part-time and get our educations. We can make a good life. We belong together, we really do."

There were some potential roadblocks in these plans, obstacles that youngsters in love weren't likely to linger over. What if, in Perth, one or more of Sorina's street customers from King's Cross were somehow to recognize her? And what if it were a thug who had a hand in the trafficking trade? I envisioned another kidnapping, this time to an antechamber of Hell, imprisoned whoredom in a filthy, smelly, bleak room entailing sickness, beatings, perversions, madness, no way out until suicide or death from some degenerative venereal disease.

"Let me ask you something, Sorina," I said.

"Yes."

"The night I found you at my front door, had you tried to commit suicide?"

"Yes."

"Why?"

"Because I wanted to die. Because I hated my life."

She started to say more, blushed, looked away for a moment, as to compose herself and resumed.

"Jake, all the things I've had to do with men for the

last six years, I hated, I never once found pleasure in being touched by any of them. Not once. But with Zeke I know what it means to love and care for someone, to be with him in all ways. I know this is dangerous, Jake, and part of me wants to run away and hide so that nobody can be hurt."

"That's not going to happen," said Zeke.

"No."

"We've made a pact to be strong, not to wimp out," Zeke said, looking at me levelly.

"So what do you think?" he said.

"I think you should look at it carefully, and then tell your parents."

14

y plan had been to surprise her with a Tarzan act—leap over the back fence, startle her, pick her up, run around grunting like an ape man.

The stroll to her place under a bright crescent moon had been pleasant but turned into something horrendous. As I neared the mansion, I saw a stocky blonde man about fifty years old scamper hurriedly out the front door, get into a Mercedes Benz and speed off. I noted the license number and abandoned the comedy plan. Something was very wrong.

The front door was unlocked, slightly ajar.

"Florence? Flo?" I called from the foyer. No answer.

"Are you here?" Still no answer. I scurried up the stairs.

A moan sounded from her room. I entered and saw her

on the bed, curled in the fetal position, a thin line of blood streaming from her nose. She was breathing, her eyes were wide open. I kneeled and murmured her name. She turned and gazed at me curiously, as an infant might look at an animal it hadn't seen before. I couldn't tell if she was in shock or under the influence of some drug. She recognized me and blinked several times.

"Jake?"

"Yes, it's me. It's Jake."

"It's you."

She reached for me, pulled me toward her, held on tightly and rocked back and forth.

"Jake."

"What happened, Flo?"

"Just hold me."

"Wait a moment." I went into the bathroom, ran some water onto a towel, returned and rinsed the blood off her face. I helped her lean forward and placed the towel under her nose, lightly pinching the nostrils. The bleeding stopped and I cleaned her face again. She began sobbing, breathing in spasmodic gasps. I lay down, put my arms around her and stayed quiet until the shuddering subsided and she relaxed.

"What happened, Flo? Who was that man?"

"I don't know. I never saw him before."

"What did he want?"

"He said he had a message from the organization. That's all he said. Then he slapped me hard, raped me, and left."

"I'm calling the police."

"No, don't. They'll come back and kill me. Look on the

dresser. He left a note."

There was a blank envelope. I opened it and pulled out a piece of paper that said: *We're not letting the girl Sorina go. Don't ever interfere with business again.*

"We have to get you to a doctor."

"No!"

"He could have infected you or torn something."

"It wasn't his body, it was that." She pointed to a rubber dildo that had been flung to the floor. "He did it with that. He had his arm on my throat so I couldn't move or scream."

"Jesus." I felt a rush of horror and loathing as though Satan himself had been in the room. A torrent of rage flooded through me and I sprang up, paced, pounded on the wall, kicked a wastebasket, yelled "sick bastards!" out the window.

Flo looked frightened, as though another madman had come into the room. Instantly, I had a flash of remorse and let up; it was she who'd been assaulted, not me.

"Well then, let's call your personal physician."

"No! And please get that thing off the floor! Throw it away, get it out of here!"

I picked up the dildo, using the bloody washcloth as a buffer, carried it downstairs and outside, and flung it into the garbage can, along with the rag.

I grabbed a stick and stirred up the garbage so that the smarmy thing was covered over. It occurred to me the perp's fingerprints may have been detectable on it, but that was an academic question now. As an experienced creep, he'd probably been wearing gloves.

Flo had recovered enough to leave the bed, run bath

water and get into the tub.

"Is it gone?"

"I got rid of it."

"Stay with me?"

"Yes."

After the bath we got into bed, tuned to some light ballad music on the radio and she curled into my arms. We slept fitfully throughout the night, waking intermittently, reaching for assurance the other was there.

15

I paid Muhammad for another month, moved out of the cottage, and in with Flo. Sydney's high society, such as it was, would have something to gossip about, which was all right, and we'd be together, an arrangement that was all right too. A large-windowed den facing the patio had excellent light and would suffice as my new studio.

My initial plan of leading a new life in Australia anonymously, painting, reading, wandering about as the world's witness, had morphed into something quite different, and a casual involvement with reality was no longer an option, or even possible. Strangely, I didn't mind.

I told Matt what had happened to Flo, and after he had a government friend check out the license number I'd seen, it was traced to an accountant named Malcolm Durvey who lived in Manly, a suburb of Sydney that juts out like a bump in the harbor. I mapped his address on the internet, took the ferry to Manly two mornings after Flo's assault and waited. Conveniently, there was a café down the street from his house, with an easy surveillance from an outside table. The Mercedes was parked in the driveway. I didn't have to wait long. In a short while a fiftiesh, portly man in a business suit emerged from the house and drove off, the same guy I'd seen exiting Flo's doorway.

On the back of a copy of the threatening note he'd left her, I penned a message, and put it into his mailbox:

We know who you are, and what you did. We know everything about the thugs you're associated with. It's all over.

I returned to the café in the evening and waited for his return. It was a longer wait than I expected. The accounting business must have been very busy. I ate a meal, drank two cups of coffee, did a thorough reading of the *Daily Telegraph*, and completed two puzzles before his car pulled up. He got out and walked up the steps to his house. In a few minutes, he came out again looking worried, holding his mail in his hand, surveying the neighborhood. I was inside the café this time, watching through a window. The cliche "white as a ghost" was an apt description of his face at the moment. On my cell phone, I called his home number, which I'd gotten from his office on an "emergency contract" ruse. It rang five times before he picked it up. I could picture him staring at it in fright.

"Hello?"

"We know who you are and who you work for. We know about the rape."

"Who, who, who, is this?" he stammered.

"Never mind who it is. If you want to live, go to the Sydney police and give them a full confession. Tell them what you did, and who put you up to it."

"I, I, I, don't know what you're talking about."

"Shut up, you filthy pig. Just do what I said." I hung up the phone.

I called his number ten minutes later, and it was busy, as I thought it would be. Talking, doubtlessly in a panic, to the scumbags who controlled him.

Next day, the morning paper carried the following item:

A drowned body identified as a well-known accountant named Malcolm Durvey was pulled from the bay water near Manly. A gunshot wound to Durvey's head indicated death by murder or suicide. It was expected an autopsy would reveal more information.

Durvey was in the spotlight two years ago during an investigation of local entrepreneurs who were suspected of violating tax laws by under-reporting the profits of various entertainment enterprises.

I was certain his employers felt he might break down and spill everything he knew, and had herefore eliminated him. I felt avenged, and wondered what I was becoming.

16

On an afternoon after I'd completed a painting to my satisfaction, and Flo was occupied with a meeting of the Historical Preservation Society, I was restless, and strolled to the Frontback to have a beer, socialize, perhaps get into a game of darts.

Except for a couple in a booth speaking in a murmur, and a young fellow playing the pinball machine, the bar was quiet. A middle-aged man who had been observing his sad reflection in the mirror shook his head, rose, and left. Martin's dour brother-in-law, Georgie, the day bartender, had nothing to say beyond, "What'll you have?" and occupied himself with the time-honored occupation of wiping cocktail glasses until they gleamed.

I was content, for the while, to sip beer and contemplate the shelf of shiny liquor bottles reflected in the long mirror.

In twenty minutes or so, a thin, bearded man maybe sixty years old, came into the bar and took the seat next to me. You're Jake Brody, aren't you?" he asked.

"How did you know?"

"I remember seeing your picture in the paper in regard to an exhibition of your work. My name, by the way, is Marvin Deskeit."

He spoke with an English accent.

"So, what do you do, Marvin?"

"Well, it's a mouthful. I'm currently visiting associate rabbi-in-residence at the Grand Synagogue of Sydney."

"That is a mouthful. What brings you to this bar?"

"Just playing hookey before a meeting. You know, it's a strange coincidence. I met your ex-wife Judith yesterday. She was on a tour of the synagogue. Spoke of her purpose in coming here, to salvage a young victim of trafficking. Mentioned you and your brother. You look surprised. Sydney is some ways a small town, and word gets around about people. What was most astonishing was, she mentioned she was the wife of Herman Bladowitz and Herman was one of my students in a yeshiva in England many years ago."

"Well, Marvin, as one hookey player to another, let me buy you another."

"Thanks, Jake, but I'll have to drink up and get over to the Opera House. Director wants to discuss ideas about authenticity in *Samson and Delilah*."

We drank quietly for a while, shook hands and he left. I left soon after.

Next morning, I got a call from a woman who identified

herself as the secretary of Kovar Petrovich. She said he wanted to meet with me at his office a block from the Grand Synagogue. I wondered if this was somehow tied in with the odd meeting with Deskeit.

"I don't know this person," I said.

"It's urgent, very urgent, please come. You'll find it rewarding."

Two hours later the secretary led me into his office. A well-dressed elderly man was sitting on a couch. He didn't rise or offer a handshake but watched me closely as I entered. He gestured toward a chair.

"Mr. Brody."

He spoke with an accent I guessed to be Russian.

"Yes. And who might you be?"

"My name is Kovar Petrovich. I want to speak of a serious matter with you regarding your family's involvement with a young woman from Romania named Sorina."

"Yes?"

"You needn't be circumspect, Mr. Brody. I'm aware of all the facts."

Petrovich looked to be about seventy years old. His well-trimmed silver hair and mustache gave him a distinguished look that was somewhat mitigated by a nose that inclined to the left, probably broken in some long-ago skirmish. He had the semblance of one of those urbane, genteel Hollywood movie villains who would slice your throat in an instant, if provoked.

"Well then, what can I do for you, Mr. Petrovich?" The formality of last names was ludicrous, with its implied respect.

"I want you to know the young woman will be released to the care of your ex-wife and brought to America. It will be arranged through the auspices of the Australian government."

He leaned forward, gazing intently into my eyes. His stare was powerful, as of one who was used to getting his way.

"There will be no reprisals against anyone who was involved in this situation."

"A woman I love was harmed in a vicious way."

"That was unfortunate, and not intended."

I didn't believe him.

"The one who perpetrated a vile act on her does not exist any more. Her estate has been restored to her, free of debt, and she won't be harassed again, as long as she lives."

"Why are you telling me all this, and what's your stake in it?"

"Come, Mr. Brody, you're an intelligent man, well educated, and an artist. Your imagination must have already filled in all the facts."

Of course it had. I knew instantly he was a bigwig in organized crime. It came off him like a dark halo.

"Then tell me this—why are you meeting with me, a rabbi, of all people?"

"For a certain reason. I was married to a Jewish woman who migrated here with me from the Soviet Union. She was a beautiful, extraordinary woman, the love of my life. She was deeply religious and her synagogue was a rich source of solace and meaning to her. She died five years ago. Over the years, I contributed many thousands of dollars to the synagogue in her name and I still do so, though I'm not Jewish myself. The matter we're discussing now is another offering in her memory. She would be pleased."

I closed my eyes for a moment to gather my reactions to this surrealistic encounter. I'd been conversing rationally with a kingpin gangster who hovered inscrutably between realms of evil and benevolence. Perhaps as a wielder of power they were equal to him. I wondered if his wife, seeing him through the prism of love, had perceived some quality that was closed off to others. Their marriage must have been one of those mysterious bondings of darkness and light that novelists like to romanticize.

But that was a mindspin. I thought of the thousands of children who had been trapped into sexual slavery at the whim of people like him and felt only revulsion. If he wanted to please his wife's ghost, why didn't he free all he could?

"So, Mr. Petrovich, when is this going to happen?"

"The appropriate papers should be issued within a week, and she'll be on her way."

"I have some questions." Among them, I wanted to know how he could bear to look at himself in the mirror.

"You're perplexed about me but there will be no revelations. Our matter is concluded and you may go now."

We nodded, I rose, and we parted without shaking hands. I'd been given the golden prize, yet I had a strong urge to get into a shower and cleanse myself.

17

First I called Flo to tell her the good news, which she told me she already knew. A bank vice president had called on her to present her with a deed free and clear to her home, in exchange for her transferring her ownership of the Fascination Club property to a certain Kovar Petrovich—which she gladly did. In addition, the comfortable monthly stipend that had been bequeathed to her in her husband's will had been cleared of debt claims and increased, with interest.

"You're free of them, Flo. And so is Sorina."

"Not only free but restored. It's like a stream has flowed through me and washed away the grime. For a time I thought your coming into my life had intensified the curse on me, but it was the opposite. Even the attack by that freak—it'll fade away. I'm grateful to you."

"Grateful isn't deserved. I've been a side character in a series of events."

"Next week, I'm flying to Switzerland, to visit with my son. Why don't you join me?"

"Switzerland. Why not? I like chocolate and I like watches. Sure, I'll join you."

"Wonderful. And there'll be things other than chocolate and watches."

"Really! I'll see you in a few hours."

I walked up the hill from downtown to King's Cross, sat at an outdoor café and ordered a coffee. It was mid-May, Spring in the United States but Autumnal in Sydney, though a blindfolded traveler would have had a hard time telling which was which. There had been a light rain in the morning, a cool breeze was rustling through the tree leaves and the sun was shining. From where I sat I could contemplate a galaxy of dust motes floating serenely through filtered rays of light.

I saw that Tuffy, the hooligan who had tried to buffalo me when searching for Sorina, was standing across the street in front of the Fascination Club. He was better dressed than before, in slacks, a white shirt and a buttoned-up vest. He'd let his hair grow back, shaved off the goatee, trimmed the sideburns, and the overall look transformed his appearance from that of a street punk to a grown man. Judging from an air of authority he exuded, I guessed he'd been upgraded to manager of the club after the guy who'd replaced Mack Ruggles. The tall transvestite I'd seen flirting with Ruggles came out of the front door of the club with an Asian girl who looked no more than sixteen years old. She was crying and talking rapidly. A balding middle-aged man, Caucasian, short and chubby, exited out the front door, though the club wasn't yet open for business. As he tried to sidle by the conversing trio, Tuffy put an arm out to restrain him and said something harsh. The man balked, Tuffy tightened his grip and jerked him a bit. He gave in, pulled out his wallet, gave Tuffy some bills, glanced from side to side, and walked off hurriedly. The girl continued to cry and chatter, and Tuffy gave an order to the transvestite, who pulled her back into the club. Tuffy lit a cigarette, scanned the street, paced for a bit and went inside. I didn't want to dwell on what had happened to the girl, or what the extra money had been given for, but I knew it had been something depressing.

Somewhere in Asia, in some remote village from where she may have been kidnapped, or sold, or offered a bogus job, her family was thinking about her, missing her, and praying she was all right. She wasn't. Like thousands of others in her predicament, she wasn't all right.

18

Sorina's path to freedom had been well paved. The necessary documents from Australia and the United States had been received, along with her airline ticket, new clothing, and a makeover by a hairstylist that gave her a chic, sophisticated look.

It had been proposed by Sarah and Matt, and agreed upon by Zeke and Sorina, that their marriage be deferred for a year, while Zeke completed his engineering degree, and Sorina began her studies at Berkeley City College. Zeke would visit her in Berkeley during mid-semester break, at the home of Morgan Hoff, who was providing his attic apartment for her.

Before she left for the states, Sarah and Matt hosted a going-away dinner party that included my ex-wife Judith and her fellow redeemer Morgan, along with myself, Flo, June,

Sorina and Zeke.

Coming face to face with Judith wasn't the awkward, unpleasant situation I'd foreseen. It had a neutral ambience, sort of like running into an old acquaintance who had long ago faded out of your life. Oddly, I felt more connected to Morgan, perhaps out of misguided pity for the fringeness in which he existed, the hopelessness I thought to be lurking beneath his positive attitude. Seated alongside June during the meal, the two of them seemed to have a unique rapport, a shared knowledge of marginality not available to the rest of us. They exchanged friendly glances along with the bread, gravy or wine they passed, and laughed when the others laughed, more in response to each other than to any jokes that were made

Before the meal, Judith had asked Flo if she could "borrow" me for a few minutes.

"Well I don't know," Flo said. "If you return him with interest then I guess it's all right."

"That shouldn't be a problem. I can see you've got his interest all the time."

They gave each other appraising looks that conveyed some essential female information, or so I assumed.

"She's lovely," said Judith, when we got to the veranda.

"Yes."

"How did you find her?"

"It's a long story, having to do with an art exhibition."

"It's strange, Jake, all those years together, and we never got to know each other in a meaningful way."

"No, we didn't, really."

"After the stillbirth, we just marked time going through the motions of a married couple," she said, "and now here's this, on another continent."

"It's weird, all right. But there's something else you wanted to talk about. Is it Sorina?"

"No, Matt filled me in on all the background, and I've had a long talk with her. She's extraordinary. Mostly, I wanted to touch bases with you, say something personal before flying away. After all, you were my husband for seven years, and that means something."

"But there's something else."

She turned away a moment, frowned, crossed her arms and turned back to me with an air of diffidence.

"The thing with Herman, it was a mistake. It hasn't been right. I fell into something like an adolescent crush and I was ecstatic to be pregnant again. But between us, on a day to day basis, it's been a disaster. We simply aren't compatible as a couple. I realized that not too long after we got married, and I thought the baby might bind us together. But that didn't happen. The baby, by the way, is a boy and very beautiful. We named him Steven."

"Congratulations on the baby, and tough luck about the marriage. What are you going to do about it?"

"I don't know. Herman's vanity is hard to abide, he's so suave, so pleased with himself. He's the world's greatest authority on everything. I guess I'm not so perfect myself. But the role of adoring wifey is what Herman was expecting, and I didn't admit that to myself. It's just not me. Maybe it could be, if we had a deep, warm rapport, but we don't."

"I don't know what to tell you. You went from one marriage in limbo to another, and now what? You know the cliché, 'get a life.' Maybe that's the answer. What life do you want?"

"I don't know, Jake. You found yours, didn't you?"

"It found me, as well. There've been a lot of surprises. Let's get back to the party, Judith."

"Yes. Thanks for our little visit."

After dinner, we had a "talent show" created out of slips of paper we'd placed in a hat and passed around. Each of us had written a performance suggestion and the rule was the getter had to do whatever was proposed. The results were entertaining, if not elegant. Morgan had to juggle two apples, June did a tap dance number, Matt had to mime shaving a customer in a barber chair, Sarah did a percussion beat on pots and pans, Zeke toed across the rug as though doing a high wire act, Sorina did somersaults, I sang a pseudo opera aria, Judith spoke in "tongues," and Flo had to read a passage from *Gone With the Wind* mimicking the Southern-accented voice of Scarlett O'Hara.

Afterward, Sarah served snifters of cognac, Matt lit some wood in the fireplace and we curled around the floor lazily, watching the flames and the glowing embers.

Sorina played some original music on her harmonica, that was steeped in melancholy.

19

Heilen, a Swiss-German word for healing, was the name of the place, an elegant sanatorium close to Lake Geneva, built in the early twentieth century, and inspired by Sigmund Freud's notions on the unconscious mind's influence on human behavior. During that era, Freud was venerated by a large segment of European intellectuals who savored the conception of the *id* as a mysterious, mischievous driving force in human affairs.

A sign above the gate said, simply, *Welcome to Heilen.* Flo announced us on the intercom, nudged me and held up crossed fingers for luck.

Dr. Skyberg, the chief psychiatrist, met us at the elaborately carved front door that resembled the entrance to a cathedral. He was Norwegian, tall, athletic-looking, perhaps thirty-five years old, slightly balding, with red hair and a cheerful demeanor. He greeted Flo cordially.

"Ms. Rinkov! Always glad to see you."

"This is my companion, Mr. Jake Brody."

"And you, sir. Good to see you too."

His handshake was strong but not competitive.

"Well? What news?" asked Flo.

"I have wonderful news, wonderful news! Your son is returning to life."

"What do you mean?"

"We're not sure whether it's the effect of treatment, or just the healing power of time, but he's gradually responding to the world around him. He allows the staff to take him for walks now, and just yesterday he went into the dining room on his own, picked up a fork and finished a meal without assistance. He then went into the social room and watched a soccer match on television, from beginning to end. It was observed he nodded to other patients, as he sat down."

Flo looked stunned. After a moment, she exclaimed, "Doctor!" and threw her arms around him.

"Yes, it's true," he said.

"I want to see him now."

"Certainly. He's in his room."

He was sitting on a stuffed leather chair, observing the garden through opened French doors.

"Jeremy," Flo said softly.

He turned slowly to look at her. His skin was pale and there were dark circles under his eyes. His brown hair had been combed neatly, and parted in the middle, by whoever had been attending him. He looked at his mother with an expression of surprise, walked to her, touched her face, stroked her hair, and put his arms around her. They stood that way for several minutes, quietly.

She said, "This is Jake, my close friend."

Jeremy looked at me curiously, and I nodded.

"I'm going to leave you alone to visit," I said. "I'll be down the hall in the social room."

There were six patients there. One, a young Asian woman, was seated cross-legged next to a large bookshelf, perusing a book of photographs. Nearby, a group of four was playing bridge at a card table, occasionally voicing triumph or chagrin at some maneuver that was inscrutable to me as a non-player. The room was brightly lit in sunlight except for a corner where green velvet curtains were drawn and a man was watching a movie on a wall-mounted television set. It was 1950's vintage, filmed in what was then heralded as glorious technicolor.

A choreographed scene involved a hundred women swimming in kaleidoscopic patterns around Esther Williams as she swam eloquently, smiling into the camera, conveying aquatic delight. The actor Van Johnson looked on admiringly, a tipoff there would be some business between them.

I sat in a stuffed chair next to the patient, who turned from the film and regarded me curiously.

"Are you a fan of these Hollywood extravaganzas?"

He was middle aged with unkempt gray and black hair that stuck out in patches like weeds. His skin was pockmarked as though his adolescent acne phase had come upon him like a plague. His green eyes peered deeply, furtively, from within their sockets.

"Sometimes," I answered. "They bring on nostalgia for a simpler, more naïve time in America."

"Simplicity and naivete. A blessed state."

"How did you know I spoke English?" I asked.

"I overheard you and your lady talking, in the hallway."

"And yourself? Where are you from?"

"I was originally a Czech, but with the great division after communism, I was categorized as a Slovak. I've applied for Swiss citizenship, but have been turned down on the grounds that I am insane. My name, incidentally, is Fritz."

"Good to meet you, Fritz. I'm Jake. If you don't mind my asking, what is it that qualifies you for insanity?"

"The documents. Long ago I bribed an attendant to sneak my medical record from the files, and I learned I was diagnosed as suffering from schizophrenic paranoia, heightened with delusions of persecution."

"That's quite a diagnosis."

"But there's more. The doctors concluded this derangement was induced by the late stage of a certain venereal disease, syphilis. After that was brought to light, medicine subdued the virus, but my central nervous system was irreversibly damaged, and here I am, hapless victim of one misguided pathetic tryst with a prostitute."

"You got a lousy deal, but since you understand the cause and effect of your problem, doesn't that allow you to stand back from it?

"Only some of the time. As for instance, right now, your insistent questions are making me very suspicious. In fact,

I'm wondering if the administration has sent you here to spy on me, and tell them what you have learned. I have no way of knowing whether I can trust you or not."

"You can trust me."

"Why should I believe that?"

I thought he might be kidding until I saw that his eyes had become wide with fear. Something in him had suddenly cried out *danger*! I had the sense that if I took the obvious route at this point, got up and walked away, it would only increase his suspicion, so I stopped talking and watched the movie.

After the aquatic spectacle, Esther Williams and Van Johnson were flirting at the edge of a hotel swimming pool. She was wearing a one-piece swimming suit on her drop-dead gorgeous body, and he was dressed in the uniform of a U.S. Army pilot, his chest bedecked with medals, his shoulders bearing the insignia of a major. Who wouldn't wish such magnificent cinema creatures the best of luck?

"I like it better when she swims," Fritz said.

His features and posture were relaxed and he seemed more or less composed. We picked up the thread of our conversation as though it hadn't been interrupted by his paranoid tic.

"The prostitute I mentioned Jake, she was hardly more than a child."

An expression of pain contorted his face. He clicked the movie onto "pause," sat back, exhaled, shook his head. I wondered why he felt I was trustworthy again, but didn't ask.

"She was working in a whorehouse on the outskirts of Bratislava, where I was employed as a lawyer. I had never had sex, and I thought it was time, so I went to this place. I chose her among the girls in the parlor because she was plainest, and I found her the least frightening. We went to a small room that smelled rank. The sheets were unwashed and crumpled, the blankets stained, the window shade was marked with graffiti. On the wall above the bed was a crucifix. A crusty towel draped on the dresser looked as though it hadn't been washed for a long time. I managed to perform the act, but it was without magic, flat and disappointing, very remote from what you would call lovemaking. Afterward, when I was spent, I felt appalled at what this girl had to do repeatedly with strangers, and my role in it. I gave her some extra money and asked if she would like to talk. She said customers often wanted to talk but she had nothing to say to them. I gave her some more money and asked her to tell me just three things: How old was she, where was she from, and how did she get to this place.

"'I'm fifteen, I'm from Poland, and I met a man who brought me here after I ran away from home,'" she said.

"'Can you leave this place?'" I asked her. She said she didn't want to talk anymore, and asked me to dress and go.

"That sad interlude was all I've ever known of physical love. I think I must have deserved the disease I caught, that it was destiny's way of teaching me about responsibility to others, about the suffering of this world."

"You can't hold yourself responsible for the suffering in this world."

Fritz' features became contorted again, and again there was fear in his eyes, then abruptly a reversal, and the tension melted away.

"Perhaps not. But I wish I was in at least a position to do something about it."

He got up and left. I saw that he walked with a slight limp, possibly another effect of the disease he interpreted as retribution.

That evening, Flo and Jeremy and I went to dinner at a French restaurant several miles from the sanatorium, though Dr. Skyberg cautioned against it.

"A sudden change in surroundings might be overwhelming for him. It's been a long time."

"My mother's intuition tells me it'll be all right," said Flo.

The doctor made a slight bow. "Mother's intuition trumps anything I might say. Forgive me."

The restaurant, Lac de Geneve, belied its name. It was off a winding road, nestled amid a grove of trees, with no view of the lake to justify the Lac part. A tall, very thin woman holding a menu greeted us effusively in French and Flo responded well enough that the two of them were able to carry on a brief, animated conversation. Jeremy glanced at me in bafflement and I shrugged, to acknowledge our mutual ignorance of French. He shrugged back, an emphatic, somewhat Gallic gesture. Flo caught it and smiled.

"You're teasing my show-offy French. Shame on you guys!"

During the meal, Jeremy participated in the conversation with occasional grunts.

"The staff neurologist said it'll be a while before his

facility with language returns," said Flo, "but he's an eloquent grunter."

He emitted three staccato grunts in response, raising an index finger pontifically. The hostess, curious about our loud guffaws, came over to see what the ado was about, and Flo reassured her that everything was all right, her son happened to be a clown.

Midway through dinner, the hostess pulled a curtain aside and a trio of musicians entered playing Gypsy tunes on a violin, concertina and mandolin, strolling from table to table, singing ballads, to the delight of the patrons. When they got to us, the mandolin player put down his instrument, took a rose from our vase and placed it in Flo's hair. He gestured toward the small dance floor, said, "madame?" and she arose and danced with him, twirling gracefully. Several of the diners applauded when she returned to the table.

"I have to say it, you've never looked more beautiful," I said. "I'm jealous of everybody who's looked at you tonight."

She took the rose out of her hair, tore some petals off, tossed them at me and Jeremy.

"Because the night is beautiful," she said.

Jeremy's eyes had become glazed and he had a look of fatigue.

"I think our celebration has tired him," said Flo. "Maybe we were out of bounds to let him have so much wine."

He shook his head "no."

His head slumped onto Flo's shoulder and he dozed, as we drove back to Heilen.

20

For several days, Flo and I left our hotel after breakfast and spent time with Jeremy at Heilen, essentially just hanging out with him. He was coming in and out of awareness, sometimes coherent though not verbal, and other times, in a fog. The day nurse had advised Flo that in the latter state, he liked to sit in the garden, on a certain bench facing the pond, and bask in the sun. One of the sanatorium's cats, an orange and white shorthair named "Lido," would join him there and administer a sort of pet therapy. The feline seemed to consider himself a member of the staff. He'd spring onto Jeremy's lap and emit abnormally loud purrs while Jeremy, a faint smile on his face, rested his hand on Lido's back and absorbed the vibes. Lido would terminate the session when he decided it was time to swat at a butterfly or chase after a panicky lizard.

Flo decided to stay at the sanatorium with Jeremy for two more weeks, then bring him home permanently to Sydney, where she would work with an array of doctors and therapists to restore him, hopefully, to his prior good health.

I wasn't significantly needed at Heilen for that period, so I elected to be elsewhere. I took a train to Paris and found a room in a small hotel on the Ile de la Cite, near Notre Dame Cathedral.

Shadows of the sort of youthful tragedy that had befallen Sorina seemed to fall darkly in every corner of the world. As I walked about Paris I saw that very young girls were selling themselves on the street as their pimps lurked in the background. It wasn't hard to recognize the pimps, they had a look and an attitude. The girls, as well as their taskmasters, appeared to have come from Eastern Europe or the Balkans. A few seemed to have been brought over from Africa. Some of them were barely more than children and the heavy makeup they wore couldn't conceal that. There was no lack of customers for them to connect with and go off with into some sordid room, parked car or alleyway.

Lust for sale was a cheerless, pathetic drama. I wanted Paris to be a noble exception, where the transformation of children into sex objects wouldn't be tolerated, but there it was, and authorities were unable or unwilling to stop it. I had rescue fantasies of rounding up the girls, putting them into a van and delivering them to some safe haven where they'd be cleansed of the squalor etched into their psyches.

With all my lofty sentiments, I realized I would probably have been as tolerant and unconcerned as the general crowd of passers-by if my life hadn't changed direction when a damaged young woman turned up at my doorstep one night.

There was more to do in Paris than brood, and I availed myself of it. It's a place to drift about aimlessly, pausing here and there to sketch fragments of scenes at cafes, public gardens, boulevards, and along the banks of the Seine. In the City of Light, dawdling is reckoned as a worthy pursuit, an interval to ponder space, time, culture, the elusive promise of grace.

On a mundane level, there were bars that offered unique conversations with people such as Reynard, a Tunisian emigre who worked as a translator. He was a roguish, clever fellow who, if he could be believed, had been a skilled and successful seducer of mature, elegant Parisian women of the sort that are called *belle*, until he underwent a shift in sensibility.

"These women who are *belle*, when you are through with the lovemaking, and the talking, and they get into the shower, everything washes off their face, and they are no longer *belle*, they are ordinary."

"Is that a serious problem?"

"I wouldn't say serious. I would say it inspired a new direction, which was to shift my attention and energies to young backpacker women from America and Scandinavia who are *jolie*, meaning pretty. *Belle* fades away but *jolie* is always *jolie*."

And there was Steffan, a Welshman, a painter obsessed with the subject of meaninglessness.

"Everything we do, everything we believe, is hollow.

There's nothing but zero behind our ideas. All the things we cherish are no more than fantasies we cling to absurdly, like shipwrecked men clinging to a plank."

"Okay, but I wonder if you could find room for doubt, concede at least some potential, some innate worth that abides in humans."

"Humans? We're a hopeless bunch of idiots befouling the universe."

"Damn! Is there anything we can do about it?"

"Drink. That's it. There's nothing else to do."

"That's it?"

"Nothing more."

We ordered another round, and cheerfully, raised our glasses to the pointlessness of human life.

21

Back in Sydney, life for the while, was like one of those cheerful picture postcards on which you write, "I'm fine, everybody's fine, hope you're fine too. Wish you were here."

It turned out things weren't so fine with Sorina. This came in the mail after she'd been in Berkeley a few weeks:

Jake, I didn't want to worry Zeke with this, and I hope you'll excuse it if my literacy is not so good, but I need to talk about this, and I thought you'd understand. After what everybody has done for me, I don't want to present negative things to them.

But I feel like I'm losing my mind sometimes because being free is very confusing to me. I haven't caught up with my new life well enough to fit in with it and I don't know who I am as a free person. I spent most of my life being an orphan or a prostitute and those things caused me to reject myself and others, which is why you found me almost dead that night.

When I was constantly with Zeke and the rest of you I felt safe, and for the first time since I can remember, I felt loved. I came out of my shell, and now I think I'm going back into it.

Although I feel grateful for everything everybody has done, I can't say gratitude is something I can draw strength from right now.

Part of the problem is that everybody here is so nice to me and I feel like a freak who it makes people feel good to be nice to. Does that make any sense? Even in my classes at Berkeley City College, the teachers and students act like I'm something special because I speak with an accent, and some of the males are wolfing after me, and I don't want that, it makes me feel cheap again, and angry.

At the synagogue, Judith's husband the rabbi introduced me during a service and then everybody clapped and kept staring at me. He didn't say anything about my life but I knew they all knew everything and I wanted to go hide but I had to smile at them and talk to them when the service was over.

It must seem selfish to you that I'm finding it hard to put up with people who are helping me, and even though I appreciate it, I can't help having these feelings, and I wonder when I am going to feel normal, just a person like others.

So I've been going to Telegraph Avenue sometimes and hanging out with the street people, you know, the ones who look raggedy and have scruffy dogs and no money and nowhere to go. I'm comfortable with them in a way I don't feel comfortable anywhere else in this city. I don't feel like a freak there, which is *funny, because they call themselves freaks.*

There's a girl named Julia whose life has been like my own in some ways. Her father left the family when she was five and her mother put her into foster care until she could take care of her again, and when she was thirteen, some of her mother's boyfriends molested her and she ran away. We understand each other and have become friends. It's nice to have a friend. I brought her home to my attic in Morgan's house, just to visit and let her have a shower and Morgan got very angry and said I couldn't bring people like that into his house anymore. When I asked why I could be there and she couldn't, because we're so much alike, he said I was starting a new life and should look forward to the future and not backward to the past. I know people have a limit to their tolerance and helpfulness, but still I was upset, and now I have a hard time relating to Morgan or even to most people who are helping me. I know this is terrible and I feel guilty about it and I wish I didn't feel this way. After all, I have been given a wonderful opportunity, and I hope I get over it.

I haven't said these things to Zeke because I don't want him or anybody in the family to worry. When I'm depressed, I think Zeke must be able to do better in life than getting damaged goods like me and I really don't want to ruin his life. The reason I'm writing to you is because I trust you and it helps to build my courage. Tonight I have to go to a dinner party at the house of Judith and Herman, and believe me, I will need courage for that because their guests will be curious about me, and I have to pull out of my fear of being a sideshow freak. Thank you for hearing me.

Immediately, I called her at Morgan's house, told her I understood what she was going through, but thought it was unfair to keep Zeke out of it.

"He cares, wants to make a life with you. It's important you call him and let him know what's going on, how you're feeling. You don't have to protect him, he can handle it."

Next morning, after Matt and I played a couple of rounds of tennis, he mentioned Sorina had called Zeke the night before, and they had talked for two hours. He said Zeke had seemed disturbed afterward. I didn't want to keep Matt in the dark, so I told him what Sorina had written about.

"Feeling objectified, disoriented. Not surprising," he said.

22

The following week, Judith called Matt from Berkeley to tell him Sorina had been missing from Morgan's house and her classes for four days, and that no one had been able to find her, including the police. Morgan had sought out her friend Julia on the Avenue, to no avail. The young people he talked to had offered tokes of marijuana, sips of wine, asked for money, insulted him or ignored him, but didn't reveal any information.

Matt called Zeke from his office and told him the disturbing news. Zeke packed a few things, went to the airport and got on a plane to San Francisco. He called his mother shortly before the plane took off, and told her he was going to find Sorina.

"Do you know what you're doing? This is crazy. Your finals are coming up. People in Berkeley are already looking for her."

"I can make up for lost time when I get back. The profs will let me. Don't worry, mom, I'll be all right. I've got to do this."

"It worries me. She could be anywhere with God knows who."

"I'll find out."

"I guess you wouldn't be who you are if you didn't go. But be careful. Keep in touch with us. Promise?"

"Promise."

After a week, he hadn't called home. And across the sea, Judith hadn't heard from him, though Zeke had called Morgan for what information he could get. Morgan's only advice was to talk to a group of youngsters who hung out near the intersection of Telegraph and Dwight Streets.

"He didn't give me an address, and never checked back with me after that," Morgan said. "I have no idea where he is."

Matt called, in a rage.

"Jake, we don't know what the hell's going on. You have a rapport with that girl. Have you heard anything at all from her?"

"Not since I talked to her after that letter."

"Jesus. This is driving us nuts. He went off half-cocked with a little cash and not much credit left on his charge card. And he missed the great news. A call came from UC Berkeley this morning. He's been given a research grant for next year in electrical engineering, but he's got to get back here and graduate."

"Look Matt, I'm worried, too. I'm going to fly over there

myself, tomorrow, and track it down."

He let out a relieved exhalation.

"Good, Jake. Track it down. And let us know what's going on, will you?"

"For sure, Matt. Don't let it get you and Sarah frantic. One way or another, it's going to get worked out."

That evening, Flo and I went to a dinner party given by a film director renowned for dramas about white people and aborigines involved in situations where dream time eclipsed ordinary reality. People would leave theaters somewhat bewildered and disoriented after seeing his films, as he probably intended.

The table talk progressed from light banter to seriousness when one of the guests, a TV producer, spoke of threats he had been getting in his email while putting together a program about runaways and street youths who were forced into prostitution.

"So? Are you going to produce it or not?" asked our host.

"I don't know. Something awful happened. One of the girls we interviewed was found on the street seriously beaten not long after we talked to her. I don't want any more of that."

The gloom of this was dispelled by the utter asininity of one of Australia's famous actors, seated next to Flo. He was exceedingly drunk, and had become a serious problem. He rose to sing a chorus of *Toora Loora Loora*, insisting we all join in, which we didn't, and then he began making lecherous advances at Flo, embracing her from behind, kissing her neck, feeling her beasts, and leaving me no choice but to pull him off her, and fling him against the wall. He took a wild punch at me, missed, lost his balance, and fell to the floor. His wife, furious, dumped a pitcher of water on his head and kicked him. The TV producer and I dragged him roughly outside and into his car as he flailed and shouted deprecations such as, "Take your hands off of me, you fucking Jews." His wife drove off with him at a tear, bruising the side of their BMW against a tree. The party broke up after that.

"Well, that's show business, folks," said our host. "At its worst."

Next morning, I was off for California to see what I could see.

The first thing I did in Berkeley, after sleeping off the jet lag and getting a meal, was to hire Harry Zanyk, a private detective I knew to be very competent. Harry had earned a Ph.D in Philosophy from UC Berkeley, tried teaching, didn't like it, apprenticed himself to a well-known investigator, mastered the trade, and went out on his own. He took cases only when his money was running low, and he had no trouble getting them. He was well known and widely sought after.

When he wasn't doing gumshoe work, he wrote abstruse books on metaphysics, which he published himself, and which very few people read. I'd known him since college when we were roommates in one of the UC dorms. After several months, he had moved out of the dorm and in with a psychologist, a Frenchwoman fifteen years older than him.

He'd started a conversation with her at a sidewalk café on the subject of "now" and she'd found his combination of brilliance and waggishness irresistible.

Twenty years down the road, I saw that fate had been kind to Harry. He was still lean and athletic; his facial features were marred only by a scar on his forehead, the result of a skirmish with a blackmailing gigolo he'd trailed.

"I've dealt with these kind of cases before," he said, "where youngsters have resistance to happy endings they don't feel they deserve, and screw up to put obstacles in the way. Of course there's more to it than that. On a subtle level, there's a kind of wisdom, an understanding that conforming to the routines and expectations of regular society can mean a shackling of the spirit. The problem is, if they settle into the outcast mode, they tend to end up as drug burnouts, jailbirds, suicides, wards of the state, colossal losers."

Harry employed one of those outcasts, Katz, a forty-year-old habitue of the avenue, as a source when he worked on local missing persons cases. Katz, who didn't use his given name of Humphrey, was the dean of streetery. A dedicated anarchist, he made a tenuous living helping people move, gathering signatures on petitions, managing the booths of street vendors who wanted time off—the sort of things that didn't entail paying income taxes to a government he scorned.

Katz knew all the permanent residents of the streets and the lore about them. He knew who was new, and what they were up to. Like Santa Claus, he knew who was naughty and who was nice. Unlike Santa Claus, his beard was black.

The Rabbi and Princess Harmonica

When Harry wanted to get in touch with him, he posted an orange sticker on a certain pole, and Katz stopped by his office. Harry paid him well for information, and Katz managed to persuade himself spy work didn't compromise his ethics.

It didn't take long to get the information we wanted. Katz shmoozed with various people and learned Julia had gone to stay with her mother in Santa Cruz and had brought a young foreign woman who was new to the street scene along with her. Youngsters on the avenue were often dubbed with nicknames and hers was Princess Harmonica. Voila! Katz had also learned that a young Australian guy had been asking questions about the foreign girl, and had been given disinformation, out of spite, by a certain creep she'd rebuffed after he made lascivious moves on her. That churlish jerk had told Zeke the Princess had been recruited by a local pimp to work as a prostitute in San Francisco's Tenderloin district, which explained where Zeke would be, and why he hadn't contacted anybody. I knew the layout of the Tenderloin fairly well, and went to the City to seek him out. Harry had gone to Santa Cruz to verify that Sorina was at Julia's house, and keep tabs on her. When and if I located Zeke, I'd drive him to Santa Cruz, and the two could get together.

I found him in less than half an hour. He was sitting on the sidewalk on Eddy Street in front of a laundromat, talking to a toothless guy who looked middle-aged, but could have been in his late thirties, given the deterioration unsavory habits and chronic neediness wreak on such people. If I hadn't been looking for Zeke I probably would have walked right on by without noticing him, giving him the social brush-off that street people usually get. He was unshaven, his hair was matted, his clothes were soiled and wrinkled.

"Zeke!"

He looked up in surprise and was speechless for a moment.

"Uncle Jake?"

"Yeah, it's me."

"What are you doing here?"

"I was looking for you."

He let out a whoop of joy.

"Well you found me." He put a hand out. "Help me up, I've got a sprained ankle."

He hugged me when he was on his feet and said, "Wow, it's you. You don't know how glad I am to see you."

"Glad to see you too. What happened to your ankle?"

"Got into a fracas last night with some guy who was trying to take my jacket. He didn't get it but my ankle got banged hard on the curb when we were wrestling."

"So what's been going on?"

"I heard Sorina was here, and I came to find her and get her out of here."

"Well here's the good news, Zeke. A friend of mine, private detective, ran it all down. She never was here. Some louse on the avenue gave you bad information, out of spite. She's in Santa Cruz, staying with her friend Julia at Julia's mother's house. We know that for sure. She's safe, she's all right. I'm sorry that creep steered you over here."

The Rabbi and Princess Harmonica

Zeke's face crumpled in grief, and he turned away, pounded the wall several times, leaned against a utility box and wept. When he recovered, he turned and faced me.

"You know, I've been looking for her in places straight out of Hell, massage parlors, seedy bars, brothels, run-down hotels, all the streets and alleys. I've been asking and watching and waiting. I was afraid I'd never find her, and I was afraid I would find her."

"Well, it's over Zeke, it's okay. Hungry?"

"I want to get to Santa Cruz."

"We'll get there. Are you hungry?"

"I could eat a horse."

"There's a nice hofbrau not far from here. Can you limp that far? Hold on to my shoulder. After we eat, I'll get you a room, so you can shave and take a shower. While you're doing that, I'll go up to Polk Street and buy you some clothes, and we'll go on to Santa Cruz. I've got a rented car."

The hofbrau didn't serve horses but they had buffalo burgers, the next best thing. The manager gave Zeke a contemptuous look when we came in, and walked toward him as if to kick him out. I stepped in front of him.

"It's okay, he's with me."

"Oh yeah? I can't imagine why."

"You don't have to imagine why."

He stood ambivalently, trying to decide his next move, waved his hand in disgust and walked off.

"So how come you were living on the street?" I asked, as we entered the freeway ramp a while later.

"I was pick pocketed my second day in San Francisco,

so no cash, no credit, no ID. I instantly became one of those guys I occasionally give a coin to."

"Did you think about going to the Australian consulate?"

"After I explained everything they would have wanted to whisk me back to Sydney, so I ruled that out."

"You're probably right. What did you do for food? Where did you sleep?"

"There are a couple of places, religious, that feed people every day. It was just a matter of waiting in a long line. I didn't want to do any begging, so I ate just the one charity meal at around noon. These church outfits are cool. There's no preaching, no strings attached, just food for the hungry. And it's not like the old movies where they feed a lot of derelict men. There are entire families lined up these days. As for sleeping, I had a hotel room my first night, before my wallet was stolen. I slept in a couple of homeless shelters the next two nights but they were bad places with bad smells, winos vomiting, fights breaking out, muggings. A guy I met on the street, an expatriate Englishman, brought me to a space he'd found under a freeway. It was okay, it was sheltered from the wind, and I covered up with a sleeping bag somebody had left there."

We drove in silence for a while. I glanced at Zeke. With his fatigue, ankle pain, weight loss, dark circles around his eyes and his crash course on dire straits, he had aged beyond his twenty years.

Halfway to Santa Cruz, I thought of Matt and Sarah fretting about him. I pulled off the freeway and handed him the cell phone Harry had provided. It would be dawn in Sydney and they were sure to be home.

"Call your parents, Zeke. They're worried."

"Yeah, I guess I should."

I got out of the car and walked around for a bit so he could talk in privacy. After several minutes he blew the horn and held the phone out the window.

"Mom wants to talk to you."

I took the phone.

"Hi, Sarah."

"I just want to say bless your soul, Jake. We're so relieved. Thank you, thank you, thank you."

"No problem, Sarah. We'll be seeing you soon."

I handed the phone back.

"Goodbye mom…I love you too."

Traffic was light, and it took just an hour and a half to get to Santa Cruz, the quaint ocean side town with its long, picturesque boardwalk. The city's downtown had been nicely restored after a devastating earthquake some twenty years before and was a gathering spot for new and old hippies, who provided local color for tourists.

I called Harry.

"You still there?"

"Still here. Meet me across the street from the roller coaster."

He shook hands avidly with Zeke after we pulled up.

"Good to meet you Zeke. You're a stand-up guy and I respect that."

He handed me a piece of paper with an address on it, and a hand-drawn map of how to get there.

"That's where she is, right now, at the mother's house. I'm glad you guys connected so easily. My work is over at this end so I'm going back to Berkeley. Good luck with whatever happens."

I handed him a wad of bills to cover our agreement. He nodded, stuffed them in a pocket and drove off.

It was a ramshackle cottage on a street six blocks from downtown. The stucco was cracked, the roof was dilapidated, there was a profusion of weeds where there had been a lawn. One of the front windows had been replaced with a sheet of plywood.

I stood by the car while Zeke knocked on the door. A gray-haired woman opened it. She had the look of an aging hippie, almost a stereotype, garbed in an ankle-length patchwork skirt and a tie-dye tee shirt. She wore her hair in a braid that went halfway down her back. Earrings in the shape of crescent moons dangled from her ears and a necklace with an occult-looking symbol was draped around her neck.

I couldn't hear what they were saying. She embraced Zeke warmly as though he were a long-lost friend and ushered him in. I heard her call, "Sorina!" In a few moments, Zeke opened the front door and waved me in. Sorina was behind him, grinning widely, her arms tight around his chest. She seemed as glad to see me as I was to see her, released her grip on Zeke and clasped me in a bear hug. Again, I was surprised by her strength.

"Jake! Jake and Zeke! You came to find me!"

"We were worried about you," I said. "People in Berkeley

didn't know where you were."

"Yes, I'm so sorry," she said.

She stepped back, turned away and clasped her head.

"I'm so sorry. I should have been more responsible. Everything just got to be too much."

"It's all right," Zeke said. "We're here and you're here. That's what matters."

She dried her tears with a cloth handed to her by Julia, who had entered the room. Julia imparted an inkling of what her mother must have looked like when young—chestnut-haired, blue-eyed, well proportioned, but there was a striking difference in their personalities. The mother came off as naturally cheerful and outgoing, while the daughter seemed indrawn and wary.

"I guess I should introduce us," said the mother, looking at me. "I'm Heather, and this is Julia."

Nods and hellos and a pause, as to wonder what next.

"Look, it's a beautiful day," said Heather. "Why don't we all take a walk to the beach?"

Which we did.

We strolled the boardwalk, rode the roller coaster, waded in the surf, lollygagged in the sand. I was wakened from a light sand nap by some itchy creature crawling up my shirtsleeve, and saw that the sun was giving way to evening. I raised up and spotted Sorina and Zeke walking hand in hand and chatting by water's edge. Above, on the boardwalk, Heather and Julia were seated on a wooden bench, listening to a group of strolling musicians who stopped intermittently so that a little girl could receive donations in a hat.

"Let's eat!" I called in each direction.

We found a semi-fancy restaurant at the end of a pier where fishing and sightseeing boats were moored. Snackwise seabirds circled overhead, landed, pecked, strutted boldly among the tourists.

In a spirit of adventure, we all ordered the specialty of the day, broiled shark steak. It wasn't bad. On the other hand, it wasn't too good, either.

We washed it down with generous libations of spirits, which combined with the strong coffee, got us giddy to the point of laughing at ripostes that wouldn't have seemed very funny, ordinarily. Heather had a hand on my thigh, during dessert, which while flattering, wasn't something I wanted to build on.

After dinner, mother and daughter walked home, and I booked two rooms in a hotel overlooking the ocean, one for me and one for Zeke and Sorina to renew their acquaintance in.

Next morning, we took Sorina back to the house, she and Zeke said their goodbyes, and we drove back to San Francisco. I went to the Australian consulate with him, to vouch for him, and a phone call to Matt affirmed his family connection in Sydney. The assistant consular was genially helpful, and issued a temporary passport so he could fly home.

24

Next day, I called Morgan, explained how things were, and asked him to relay to the Social Outreach Committee that Sorina was all right, and would be staying in Santa Cruz until Zeke returned to Berkeley, where family and friends would assemble for a wedding ceremony. Morgan received the news graciously, perhaps glad to be free of the kindly provider role.

On the plane to Sydney, Zeke and I ate, read, napped, watched the movie, and didn't talk much. Allowing for vagaries of fate, matters seemed to have been resolved, and there was no need to carry on about them, no need to churn the plot and tempt the Devil.